Dedication

This book is dedicated to my wife Pat and my immediate family. For my wife, Thank You for putting up with me every day. For my children and their spouses; Christina and Tom, Michael and Renee, Steven and Faith and of course, my grandson Luke. For the animals; Bob and Don, "the goats" and to Milo the wonder dog. I Love you all dearly. Thank you so much for having the faith in me when I lost the faith in myself so many years ago.

To my Dear Friend and accomplished author, Jean Lynch. I never could have completed it without you! Thank you for the editing, proof reading and commentary that helped me get this off the ground! How would I ever know that the little girl on Stephens Place would one day help me to become an author.

Disclaimer

This is a work of fiction. Names, characters, businesses, places, events and incidents are either the products of the author's imagination or used in a fictitious manner. Any resemblance to actual persons, living or dead, or actual events is purely coincidental.

Contents

The Trial - Day One

It was about a three-hour drive from where we lived in New Jersey to the Courthouse. Add in some traffic, and we're looking at four hours. I told my wife to be ready to go by 4:30 a.m. I will be sitting in the driveway with the car running.

Today is my big day. I am finally going to confront those bandits from Pluriman Insurance that took my disability benefits away! I had worked all of my life never expecting to use Disability benefits, but in March 2018, I suffered a stroke a week before my retirement. My life would never be the same.

I put on my best corporate suit that had been hanging in the closet for some time now. I remember my lawyer asking me to dress appropriately but not to overdo it. "The Jury will be looking at you all of the time. The Jury will be looking at the way you're dressed, your posture, your facial expressions and they will scan the Courtroom to see if they can spot your wife," he assured me. He said that these impressions can greatly affect the way that the Jury views the case.

At 4:20 a.m., I was loading up the car with our luggage. My lawyer told me to bring enough clothes for a week, which meant one bag for me and four for my wife. At 4:30am sharp, I was in the driveway with the car running, just like I promised. I am a stickler for being on time and even ahead of time. My wife set the house alarm, locked the front door and hurried to the car.

"This is going to be a long day" she said. "Can we stop and get coffee somewhere?" she begged.

"No time" I said. "We'll see when we get there," I finished.

As I backed out of the driveway, we turned right and headed for the Garden State Parkway. This should get us there on time I thought.

My wife said, "Do you have the directions?"

"You're asking me now?" I inquired. "They're in my phone."

"Oh God, here we go. You and that stupid phone." She answers.

"I know but it will get us there" I responded.

As I merged onto the Parkway, I could see that traffic was moving at a pretty good clip. I am a middle lane driver and the cars it the fast lane were going at least 80 miles an hour. I turned on the radio to listen for the traffic reports and everything appears to be clear sailing.

I said to my wife, "Would you like me to pull into a rest stop to get you some coffee?"

"No. It's disgusting with all those people going in there. I'll wait." she said.

"Ok, just trying to be nice" I replied.

My wife had her eyes closed and I think she was trying to sleep or avoid talking to me. I kept thinking about the trial and the events that were about to take place. It's been a long time since I've been in a Courtroom. My lawyer was very good at prepping me for everything that would transpire. But I was still nervous.

As the sun started coming up, rain drops started to appear on my windshield. Another rainy day. That means bad luck to some people but at this point, I just want to get to the Courthouse.

After about an hour, my wife opens her eyes and asked, "Are we there yet?"

"No, only about halfway" I said.

"What do you think will happen today?" my wife asked.

"Not a whole lot except my testimony" I said.

"Are you nervous?" she asked.

"Yes, a little. As my lawyer says, just tell the truth and you will be fine. He also said my case seems to be open and shut. The Defense doesn't have a whole lot going for them. Do you think I look Ok," I inquired.

"You look fine" she said.

I don't think another word was said until we reached the Courthouse.

"Look at that. We're here an hour ahead of schedule" I exclaimed.

I pulled into the courthouse parking lot and got a prime parking place. Things were starting to look up. This also means that there's nobody here.

We got out of the car and walked quickly toward the Courthouse and the rain seemed to be subsiding. Once inside, I knew that we needed to report to Courtroom 3A but before we could go any farther, we had to go through security. It was very much like airport security and we went right through.

As we arrived at the third floor, there were Court Officers stationed along the huge hallway.

"May I ask which courtroom you are looking for?" the officer asked.

"Yes, I am the Plaintiff in a case involving the Pluriman Insurance Company. The letter I have here said that I should report to Court Room 3A" I said politely.

"Thank You Sir, may I see that letter please?"

After looking at it, she said, "right down the hallway here to your right."

"Thanks" I said.

My wife and I walked down the hallway and made a right the court Room. The entire place was empty except for my lawyer, who was reading the newspaper at the Plaintiff's table.

4

I said to my wife, "Will you be Ok here? I want to go talk to Mitch for a few minutes."

"Sure, go ahead" she said. "Good Luck!"

I stood there for a minute admiring this grand institution. The Courtroom was filled with portraits of prior Judges, I assume. The windows had long red velvet drapes and the woodwork was mahogany and cherry throughout. What a daunting place.

As I glanced over at my lawyer I thought, he looked old and he makes me as nervous as a whore in church, as my old boss used to say. Why does he wear sweaters that button in the front instead of suits? Maybe that's part of his strategy but for the life of me, I didn't understand it. His name is Mitchell Sildman and I picked him because I heard that he's the best. A decision I hope not to regret, like a marriage proposal.

As I approached the Plaintiff's table I said "Hi Mitch, how are you today?"

He asked me "Ready to fight the good fight?"

"I'm ready" I said, like a proud husband to be.

My God, how did I get here? I have been in courtrooms before but mainly for Jury Duty. Now it's my turn as the Plaintiff. We are going to get these corporate bastards and get my disability reinstated. It's disgusting that it had gone this far and taken so many years for justice to be served. As my lawyer told me, "It is very unusual that these types of cases go to court. They are usually settled and the whole thing just goes away".

I really didn't give a shit because I was retired and I had nothing to do. If you want to go to court, Ok I'll go to court. I'll play your silly ass game. Better than just sittin' home looking at the four walls, I convinced myself.

My lawyer leaned over to me and asked "Do you remember everything we rehearsed? Remember don't add anything more to your response. Only a short quick answer to the question that the Defense Attorney asks".

"Got it" I said, like a pro.

"I want you to be calm and cool-headed. The Jury will be evaluating you every minute of the day" my attorney advised.

Slowly but surely the Defense lawyers began to pile in. Each one of them had their brief cases and case folders. I have nothing except Sildman. Great!

I kept glancing over at the Defense table, I thought, why does the Defense have so many people? I guess there one for each part of the case. I didn't like the looks of any of them in their suits. I'm sure they brought the "A team" to this game. We should just pack it in now. But wait, I'm only in this for 33 1/3 if we win. If we lose, oh well, no more disability, I thought.

I looked back into the courtroom and saw my wife. Of course, none of the kids showed because it may interrupt their extremely important lives. My lawyer leans over again and declared, "Buckle your seatbelt, here we go!"

In comes the Bailiff, the Court stenographer and the Jury. It also looked as though there were other Jury members sitting in the Courtroom.

The Bailiff announces, "All rise. The Honorable Douglas Bradford is presiding. Please be seated". The Judge walks in, sits down. I don't know if I like this guy or not. He looks kinda mean. Good thing I wasn't on trial for a criminal offense, I told myself.

The Jurors were seated in the Courtroom ready for "voir dire". In others words Jury Selection for the most promising jury to deliver a fair and honest decision. The Defense went first and starts eliminating Jurors.

"What the hell is happening," I whispered to my lawyer.

"We discussed this; they are selecting the Jury members that will most likely return a favorable verdict" Sildman replied firmly like a scolding professor.

"What are we going to do?" I asked in earnest.

"I paid people to provide me with the most favorable profile for us. Don't worry we'll be up next. We are trying to get older, possibly disabled folks or those who have received payments from an insurance company. Don't worry" Sildman replied firmly.

As the Defense rested, it's Sildman's turn at bat. Thank God he's wearing a suit today. The only thing I kept hearing was "Juror Excused, Juror Excused, Juror Excused. Finally, after a half hour Sildman said, "No more challenges, Your Honor."

"Thank You Mr. Sildman" the Judge replied.

"Are both parties ready to begin?" the Judge inquires.

"Yes, Your Honor" Sildman responds.

"Yes, Your Honor" the Defense replies.

The Judge started by dismissing the rest of the Jurors who were seated in the Court. After they leave, he then began administering the oath to all of those involved in the case. Then the Judge continued to address the Court.

"Ladies and Gentlemen, the Plaintiff in this case, Mr. William Lindstrom; seated at the table over there, Mr. Lindstrom would you please raise your hand to identify yourself to the Court? Mr. Lindstrom, the Plaintiff in this case contends that the Pluriman Insurance Company willfully and unlawfully discontinued his disability insurance payments in direct violation of ERISA Law 13:15:27 stating that disability payments are not to be discontinued unless there is a clear violation of the insurance contract. To be specific, ERISA stands for the Employment Income Retirement Security Act of 1974. It is a federally enacted law designed to protect the interests of employees and their beneficiaries who are enrolled in employee benefit plans, and to ensure that employees receive the pensions and group-sponsored welfare benefits that have been promised by their employers. In many cases, employers sign a contract with a 3rd party insurance company to provide benefits to the employee in case of an accident or injury. That's the law lesson for the day. Now to continue, the Plaintiff alleges that the insurance company, Pluriman Insurance, closed his case and discontinued his payments because he requested a postponement for a doctor's visit due to theCovid-19 pandemic. The Plaintiff further acknowledges that he did not refuse the Doctor's appointment but instead request a postponement until a vaccine was readily available. Is that an accurate description gentlemen?"

"No, Your Honor that is not correct" as David Rosen, the Lead Defense attorney roses. "Our company's policy clearly states that if a client will not attend a physician's appointment as directed, it will constitute a refusal and therefore a cancellation of the disability contract."

"Do you agree with that Mr. Sildman?" the Judge asked as he looked directly at my attorney.

"No, I do not your Honor. The Covid-19 pandemic has presented all of us with unique circumstances that require us to protect ourselves and our families from the transmission of this very dangerous virus. All that Mr. Lindstrom was requesting was a postponement until a vaccine could be administered. Does that seem unreasonable You Honor?" Sildman asked the Judge.

The Judge replied sternly, "Sir, I will not answer that question. That is for the Jury to decide. We are getting into the details of the case and I am only trying to summarize the situation in layman's terms."

Sildman responded again, "Your Honor I would also like to add that the Pluriman Insurance Company has well documented procedures for their employees to follow in relation to the Covid-19 pandemic, however, they have provided no guidance whatsoever for their Clients."

David Rosen, the Lead Defense attorney, rose quickly to his feet from his seat and protests loudly, "Objection Your Honor. We are under no obligation to provide medical advice to our Clients. Furthermore, we have recommended that all clients adhere to federal, state and local regulations and follow official guidance published by the Centers for Disease Control."

Sildman voiced his concern, "Objection Your Honor" The Defense did not provide any such information when it was specifically requested during Discovery."

Is that true, Mr. Rosen?" the Judge inquired.

"Your Honor I am unaware of any specific request from the Plaintiff regarding our internal Covid-19 policies" Rosen retorts.

"Ok, enough from both parties. I'm sure these subjects will be covered at length during the course of these proceedings. I will ask that we move on to Opening Statements" the Judge stated, like a mediator.

I thought Holy Shit, at this rate, we will be here for weeks.

Now the opening statements for the Jury began. There he goes as he approaches the Jury panel. My God, my lawyer looks like Mr. Rogers, sweater, sneakers and all.

"Ladies and Gentleman of the Jury. I'd like to first thank you for being here and giving up your important time to hear the case that my client has brought against the Pluriman Insurance Company. You will see that it is a very simple case. My client, Mr. Lindstrom, seated at the table there, was disabled due to a stroke he suffered in March of 2018. You will see that my client has been gainfully employed his entire life and has never been hospitalized until this incident. You will also hear that the Pluriman Insurance Company's Doctors clearly stated that this was a rare condition. The type of stroke that my client suffered is technically called a lacunar infarction of the thalamus. In laymen's terms, that means that two blood vessels exploded in the thalamus, both right and left side, which is deep within the brain. This left him with double vision which is called diplopia, severe fatigue and cognitive and comprehension issues which you will hear about in the course of this trial. My client was entitled to 5 years of disability payments according to the Pluriman Group Policy which covered him. At the time of disability, my client was employed and fully covered by this policy. After 1 ½ years, the insurance company decided that they needed to drop Mr. Lindstrom from their payment ranks, he said."

"Objection Your Honor," Rosen exclaims.

"Sustained" The Judge replied.

Sildman responded "I'm sorry, let me rephrase that statement. In March of 2020, the Pluriman Insurance Company changed its definition of disability and in August of 2020, the Insurance Company requested that my client see an Ophthalmologist. You will hear from Medical Doctors that my client's injury was not an eye disease, but rather a condition that exists in the brain. You will hear testimony that confirms that all the medical experts will agree to this."

"Objection You Honor" Rosen exclaimed., "No such evidence has been presented and a suggestion that all are in agreement is premature," he finished

"Sustained. Please be careful Mr. Sildman" The Judge instructed.

Sildman replied sheepishly "I'm sorry your Honor, I would like the record to reflect that strokes are generally classified as injuries to the brain. You will hear that Mr. Lindstrom went to weekly rehabilitation sessions at Kessler Institute and kept all of is appointments with Kessler and his recommended physicians. As we are all concerned about the Covid-19 pandemic, Mr.

Lindstrom and his wife strictly adhered to the Governor of New Jersey's regulations for lock down. In addition, I must note that my Client is in the category of high-risk people for contracting Covid-19 having high blood pressure and being in an age group that is over 65. My client simply requested a delay in the appointment until he received a Covid-19 vaccine. Because of this request he was dropped and his case closed."

"Objection, Your Honor. We conducted a full evaluation of his case before discontinuing benefits" Rosen said while barely looking up from his yellow notepad.

"Overruled." The Judge replied.

Sildman continued, "My client was dropped as noted. Today we are asking that my client be paid for the back payments and his unpaid disability payments be restored. Nothing more. Nothing less. We are not seeking substantial damages of any type. I hope you will all see the injustice that has occurred here and the fact that the Pluriman Insurance Company violated the ERISA Law which was designed to protect clients such as mine. In the name of fairness and for those who are disabled, I hope that you return a verdict in favor of my client. Thank you very much!"

"Would the Defense like to address the Jury?" the Judge asked.

"Yes, your Honor" David Rosen replies.

The Lead Defense attorney walked toward the Jury booth.

"My name is David Rosen and I am the Lead Defense Lawyer in this trial. We are extremely sorry for the stroke that Mr. Lindstrom has suffered and have supported him and his family by providing monthly disability payments to supplement his income. In addition, our Company provided monthly cash payments in the amount of $6300 per month to compensate him for the loss of income. The only thing that we asked is that Mr. Lindstrom attend scheduled doctor appointments so we could better understand his condition and provide the help he needed. According to our contract which was signed by Mr. Lindstrom on September 20, 2018, Mr. Lindstrom was required to attend all Doctors' visits scheduled at our request. The fact that Mr. Lindstrom refused…..," he stated before being interrupted.

Sildman exclaimed" Objection, Your Honor. My client never refused to attend the doctor's appointment."

"Sustained" the Judge replied.

Rosen added, "I'm sorry Your Honor but we interpret a postponement as a refusal to attend an appointment."

"Overruled" the Judge exclaimed." Interpretations do not override the law," he finished like a robot.

Rosen continued, "The Jury will also see that Mr. Lindstrom can be gainfully employed which is in accordance of our disability contract. Furthermore, we would also like to note that Mr. Lindstrom is fully capable of living a full and productive life and does not require disability payments. You will also see that our request for Doctors visits will confirm this and we are acting strictly in accordance with our contract and policies. We hope that you will respond in favor of the Pluriman Insurance Company and that both parties can resume normal living. Thank You very much."

I wasn't impressed. They didn't do a good job in convincing the Jury. Ours was much better that theirs, but I decided to see what happened next.

"The plaintiff would like to call its first witness in this case. Mr. William Lindstrom," Sildman announces.

I walked up slowly and seated myself in the witness box next to the Judge. The Bailiff administered the oath. The Judge is peering at me, why is he doing that, I thought.

"Mr. Lindstrom can you state your name and address for the court please?" Sildman asks.

"Sure, my name is William Lindstrom and I live at 404 Long Beach Boulevard in Barnegat, New Jersey," I replied like I'd been doing this my whole life.

"Mr. Lindstrom can you tell the court how many members in your family?" Sildman inquires.

"Sure, there is my wife Mary and we've been married for 44 years; we have three grown children and one grandchild," I stated.

"Mr. Lindstrom can you please tell the court what you did for a living prior to your stroke," Sildman asks.

"Sure, I was an Asset Manager for a Life Insurance Company and prior to that I was a Vice President for a three-million-dollar Consumer products company," I replied.

"Well Mr. Lindstrom, you must be pretty well off financially," Sildman smirked.

"Not really". (chuckles could be heard from courtroom). "I felt that it was very important to pay for my children's college education and that's what I did. Tuition, housing, books, meals the whole shebang." (courtroom chuckles again), I told him

"Thank You Mr. Lindstrom. How long have you suffered from hypertension which is referred to as high blood pressure," Sildman asked.

"Approximately 30 years" I responded.

"How was this problem discovered," he asked me.

"During an annual physical," I said.

"So, you regularly went for annual physicals," Sildman inquired.

"Objection, Your Honor. This is not relevant to the case" the Defense attorney alleges.

"Sustained," the Judge replied.

"Ok Mr. Lindstrom, how did you manage your high blood pressure?" Sildman asked.

"My doctor prescribed medication which I take daily" I said.

"How often do you see your doctor, Mr. Lindstrom," Sildman inquired.

"Pretty much on an annual basis for my physical or I will make an appointment if I'm not feeling well," I replied.

"A year is a long time, what did you do in the interim?"

"I purchased a blood pressure cuff and I would record my numbers every day. If I saw that they were going up, I would call my Doctor for an appointment. I attested.

"Have you seen any cardiologists since the time this condition was discovered," I was then asked.

"Yes, my internist recommended that I see a cardiologist regularly" I replied.

"How often is regularly, Mr. Lindstrom," Sildman asked.

"At least twice a year unless I don't feel well," I replied.

"Mr. Lindstrom have you had any diagnostic tests for your condition," Sildman asked.

"My high blood pressure," I asked.

"Yes Sir," Sildman responded.

"I have had stress tests where you run on the treadmill and they monitor your heart's vital signs. I've had Thallium stress tests where they inject a chemical to put your heart under stress and I have also worn a heart monitor which detects any changes in the heart rate," was my answer.

"Mr. Lindstrom, how many days of work did you lose to your condition" Sildman asks.

"None Sir, I have had an exemplary attendance record" I replied firmly, like a champ.

"Mr. Lindstrom have you ever been hospitalized because of your high blood pressure," he asked.

"No Ssir" I said.

"Have you ever been hospitalized for any reason at all," Sildman asked.

"No Sir, not until I had my stroke two years ago," I replied.

"Prior to your stroke have you ever applied for disability," he continued.

"No Sir," I responded.

"Have you ever applied for Workmen's Compensation," he asked.

"No Sir," I said.

"Have you ever been sick," (courtroom chuckles could be heard) he asked.

"Other than the occasional cold, no that's about it," I replied.

"Mr. Lindstrom, let me change things up a bit, how many types of doctors have you seen since your stroke in March, 2018," I asked.

"Let's see, I've seen neurologists, Cardiologists, psychiatrists, ophthalmologists, neuro ophthalmologists, neuro surgeons and internists. Oh yes, I also went to rehab for two months," I stated.

"Thank You Mr. Lindstrom. May I also ask if you have ever changed an appointment or requested a postponement to an appointment," Sildman inquires.

"No sir I haven't," I assured him.

"Objection Your Honor. Let the record show that Mr. Lindstrom requested a postponement of an appointment with our ophthalmologist. This request was put in writing by Mr. Lindstrom and sent to our company. This has been entered into evidence as Exhibit D1," he said.

"Sustained," said the Judge, again like a robot.

Sildman responded, "Objection Your Honor, my client requested a delay until after a Covid-19 vaccine was available to the general public. This fact is stated in Exhibit A1 dated September 11, 2020 from my client, Mr. Lindstrom to the Pluriman Insurance Company.",

The Judge asked, "May I see Exhibit D1 please? And provide a copy to both the plaintiff and defense. Gentlemen, you are both correct and therefore I will read aloud Mr. Lindstrom's letter dated, ummm let's see, August 6th, 2020. "This letter is addressed to the Client Services Representative at Pluriman Insurance and I will read it verbatim. "Dear Client Services Representative; My wife and I discussed your request to be examined by an ophthalmologist during the next 8 weeks. We do not think it is prudent to risk my health due to a possible exposure to Covid-19. In addition, I am in the age group which is highly susceptible to a possible infection. I would be willing to be examined after a vaccine is disseminated to the public and at a time when we would feel it is safe."

"Furthermore, I would like to note that I suffered a "brain injury" which has been clearly documented on MRI's. I am not sure what purpose an Ophthalmic examination serves other than for you to find a reason to discontinue my disability benefits."

That is the end of the letter. Mr. Sildman, please resume your line of questioning" The Judge stated.

"Thank you, Your Honor. Mr. Lindstrom, excluding this one-time as noted in your letter, have you ever cancelled, postponed or requested a change to any of your doctor's appointments since the time of your stroke," he asked me.

"No Sir I haven't" I replied.

David Rosen rose from his chair and said, "Objection Your Honor. We have documentation from the Social Security Administration, Exhibit D12, showing that Mr. Lindstrom requested a one-week delay in an appointment with a state authorized ophthalmologist."

"Is that true, Mr. Lindstrom?" the Judge inquired.

"Partially, Your Honor, but I must explain that the State makes the appointments without input from me. At the time that they called, my wife and I were in Florida. I couldn't possibly do it within two days because it was in New Jersey. We had driven to Florida because we were afraid to fly due to Covid-19. I asked for the next available appointment which was the following week," I explained.

"OK thank you Mr. Lindstrom I don't see this as a request for delay but rather a scheduling conflict," the Judge replies.

"Mr. Lindstrom let's go back to my original question," Sildman requests.

"No, I...," I said before being interrupted.

"Please wait until he asks the question, Sir" the Judge requested.

"I'm sorry Your Honor," I replied.

Sildman started again, "Mr. Lindstrom, let me rephrase the question to avoid these unnecessary interruptions. Since your stroke of March 25th, 2018, how many different doctors have you seen related to this incident?"

"Fourteen," was my answer.

"On what dates did you attend Rehabilitation and what was the name of the institution," he asked.

"It was Kessler Rehabilitation located in Chester, New Jersey. I went twice a week from April 24th to June 8th", I answered.

"Did you successfully complete the program," Sildman asked.

"No, Sir, I was notified that the insurance company money had run out and my treatment ended," I informed him.

"Did you feel like the treatment worked," he asked me.

"Objection, Your Honor, this question is irrelevant," Rosen exclaimed.

"Sustained," replied the Judge.

"OK, did the clinicians feel that you needed more rehabilitation," he questioned.

"Objection, Your Honor. Feelings are not admissible," Rosen stated.

"Sustained," the Judge stated robotically.

"OK, did your rehabilitation indicate, in any way, that more treatments would be required to complete the program," Sildman inquired.

"Yes Sir, he specifically told me that I should be receiving another two months of treatments to complete the agenda," I replied.

"Who is "he" Mr. Lindstrom," he inquired.

"I'm Sorry, his name is Douglas Dower. And his title at Kessler is Clinical Director. He was director of brain injury rehab at the time," I told him.

"A few more questions if I may? Do you take any medications on a daily basis to treat your condition and could you tell the Court what they are," he inquired.

"Sure" I said "metoprolol and amlodipine to control the blood pressure, simvastatin for cholesterol, and an aspirin to thin the blood," I replied.

"Mr. Lindstrom, how long have you been taking these medications," he asked me.

"Pretty much for 30 years except for metoprolol. I had been taking Lisinopril but experienced an angioedema in February 2019," I explained.

"Can you tell the court, in layman's terms, what an angioedema is," he asked me.

"Sure, it is an allergic reaction which may be life threatening because of swelling in the face and throat," I told him.

"Thank you. One final question; over the past two tears on disability, have you ever had to pay Pluriman Insurance back with any money that you received from Social Security," he asked.

"Yes, per the contract I signed with Pluriman, I was required to pay them everything that I received in settlement from Social Security," I informed him.

"May I ask what that amount was," Sildman inquires.

"Yes Sir, I paid them every penny of my Social Security settlement which was $59,575.40, which I paid on October 16, 2020. Could I get some water please," I retorted.

"The court will recess for 15 minutes for a quick bathroom break. I expect everyone to be back in their seats by 10:15, no exceptions" the Judge announces.

There were all types of mumbling and grumbling in the courtroom. My lawyer approached me and asks "Do you need to use the restroom because you need to use one that is separate from the other people in the court," he explained.

"No, but can I go talk to my wife," I asked.

"No, I'm sorry you can't," said Sildman.

"How are we doing so far," I asked.

"It's going like I expected," Sildman replied.

"I can't stand all of these objections. It's really slowing things down" I said.

"My friend, some of the questions I ask are on purpose, so I get the Jury to think about it. I may look dumb, but I'm not stupid," he told me.

Ahh then I got it. At this rate we'll be here for weeks, I thought to myself.

"There aren't too many witnesses, so things will pick up. The Judge will get antsy and start to lose his patience if it's going too slow," Sildman advises.

Everyone files back into the courtroom and took their seats.

"May we continue, Your Honor," asks Sildman

"Yes, please proceed," the Judge stated.

"Mr. Lindstrom, are you dependent on your disability payment to make ends meet," I was asked.

"Objection, Your Honor. The plaintiff's attorney is leading the witness," Rosen claimed.

"OK, let's try again. Do you require monthly disability payments from the Insurance Company to meet your financial obligations," he asked.

"Yes, sir I do," I replied. "Who doesn't?"

"Can you tell the court how much you had been receiving from the insurance company prior to them dropping you?"

"Yes sir, it was $6291.00 which is approximately 50 percent of my annual salary," I replied.

"Mr. Lindstrom, by contract, how many years was the insurance company required to pay you," he asked.

"Objection Your Honor. There is no contractual requirement to pay a person for a certain number of years" Rosen stated.

"Overruled," the Judge replied.

"According to the contract, the Insurance company was to pay me for five years" I said.

"And how long did they pay you before you were dropped?" Sildman asked.

"Approximately two years" I replied.

"Thank You Mr. Lindstrom. One more question if I may," he stated.

"Sure," I said.

"Is it true that you received Social Security Disability in May of 2020 following a Court Hearing," Sildman asked.

"Objection, Your Honor, relevance," Rosen once again questioned.

"I'll allow it, go ahead and answer the question, Mr. Lindstrom," the Judge answered.

"Yes, I was granted Long Term Disability from Social Security in May of 2020 following a court hearing" I replied.

"So, you met Social Security's criteria for Long Term Disability," Sildman asked.

"Objection," stated Rosen.

"Sustained," the Judge replied.

"Thank you. No further questions You Honor" he said as he walked toward his seat.

Okay, then came that nasty looking bastard.

"Good Morning Mr. Lindstrom, my name is Frank Delgado and I am one of the Defense attorneys seated at the table here. We would just like to expand on some of the issues your attorney has raised here. Is it true Mr. Lindstrom that you own two homes, one in Barnegat New Jersey and the other in Florida?"

"Yes, Sir, that is correct," I said.

"Do you have a mortgage on either of your homes," he continued.

"Objection. Irrelevant to the case," exclaimed Sildman.

"Sustained," the Judge answered.

"Mr. Lindstrom, what type of fees do you pay on a monthly basis for your Florida home," he asked.

"We have a mortgage which included homeowners' insurance and taxes as well as monthly water & sewer bills and electric. We also have HOA fees," I answered.

"Mr. Lindstrom, could you clarify what HOA fees are and what HOA stands for," Delgado inquired.

"Yes, it stands for Home Owners Association which is a group of residents who run the community. The HOA fee it is a monthly amount that we pay to maintain the community such as grass cutting, security and access to amenities such as the Social Hall," I replied.

"Mr. Lindstrom, is this a gated community with security guards," he inquired.

"Yes, it is," I replied.

"Sounds nice. I'd like to get a place like that someday. At your New Jersey home, is it also a gated community," he asked.

"Yes, it is," I said.

And do you also pay HOA fees," he inquired.

"Yes, we do," I replied.

"What do the fees cover," asked Delgado.

"Grass cutting, snow removal and the Clubhouse," I informed him.

"Does the Clubhouse have a swimming pool," he continued his questioning.

"Objection Your Honor, not relevant," said Sildman.

"Ok, Thank you, Mr. Lindstrom. May I ask what you sold your last house for," he asked.

"Objection you Honor" Sildman exclaims.

"Sustained," said the Judge.

"Thank you, Your Honor. I would like to introduce one of my associates, Richard Cornell who will ask you a few questions about your work history," he stated

"Good Morning Mr. Lindstrom, my name is Richard Cornell and I'll be asking some questions about your employment history. Ok, let's get started. Mr. Lindstrom How many full-time jobs have you had in your lifetime," he started his questioning.

"Three," I said.

"Could you tell the Jury the type of work you performed and the duration of each," asked Cornell.

"Sure, the first was at a paper company, do you need the name and address," I asked.

"No, the type of Industry will be fine," Delgado replies.

"I started in the mailroom and I was employed by them for 14 years," I informed him.

"And why did you leave, Sir?" Delgado asks.

"The company moved to Tennessee and I was unable to move because my mother-in-law was ill. My next job was for a consumer products company. I started as a Project Manager and left after 18 years. My title was Global Vice President," I replied.

"Wow, that's a terrific career. I guess you made a lot of money in those later years," he asked me.

"Objection, not relevant," declared Sildman.

"Sustained," said the Judge.

"Did you leave that job on your own Mr. Lindstrom, asked Cornell.

"No, I was let go," I said.

"What were the circumstances surrounding your dismissal," he asked.

"Objection, once again, not relevant," Sildman responded.

"Overruled, I'll allow the Plaintiff to answer the question. Go ahead Mr. Lindstrom," he said

"The CEO of the company asked me to do something illegal and I refused," was my reply.

"And what specifically did he ask you to do," Cornell asked.

"Objection Your Honor. I would like to approach the bench," requested Sildman

"Granted," the Judge responded.

My attorney and the two defense attorneys approach the Judge.

My attorney said quietly, "Mr. Lindstrom sued his company because of this situation and settled with his former employer. As part of the settlement agreement, he is not permitted to discuss the details."

"Gentlemen," The Judge looks directly at the defense attorneys.

"We will withdraw the question, Your Honor," Rosen states.

All parties except the Defense Lawyer returned to their seats.

"Let the record show that the defense has withdrawn their question," the Judge stated.

"Mr. Lindstrom, you previously stated that you had never collected disability prior to your health incident in March of 2018. Is that correct Sir," Cornell asks.

"Yes, it is," I replied.

"Did you collect Unemployment benefits when you were dismissed," he asked.

"Objection, Your Honor. Once again irrelevant" Sildman states.

"Overruled. Please answer the question Mr. Lindstrom."

"Yes, Sir, I did collect Unemployment," I replied.

"Can you tell the court how much you collected from the State on a monthly basis?" Cornell asked.

"Objection Your Honor, I would like to approach the bench" Sildman exclaimed.

"Ok," the judge says in seeming disgust. "What now, the Judge asked.

"The continuing questions regarding Mr. Lindstrom's income or how he spends his money are irrelevant to these proceedings. I would like to ask the Defense to cease and desist on all further questions related to monetary income," my attorney stated.

"Mr. Rosen, what do you have to say," the Judge asked.

"Your Honor, the Defense feels strongly that the Plaintiff's means of support are directly related to the financial obligations our client has to the Plaintiff," he replied.

"I'm not sure about this. Let's take a brief recess, so I can research it," the Judge stated.

Finally, the Judge announces, "The Court will recess for lunch. I will expect everyone to be in their seats by 1:00 pm. And let me remind the Jury that they should not be discussing this case over lunch. Do I make myself clear?"

"Yes, Your Honor," is heard from the Jury box in unison.

"Can I leave the stand now, Your Honor," I asked the Judge.

"Yes, you may and you are free to discuss the case with your attorney," he told me.

"Thank you, Your Honor" I replied.

I returned to the Plaintiffs table and sat next to my Lawyer. I leaned over and whispered. "How do you think it's going?"

"It's going," he said. "I don't know where they are going with their line of questioning but I think that they want to show the Jury that you really don't need this disability income. He's softening them up to show that you are rich and your one of those money grabbers," he continued.

"But, I'm entitled to it," I said.

"I know that, you know that and the Defense knows that, but the Jury doesn't. They have strange methods to convince the Jury otherwise," my attorney said.

"This isn't about me but all the others that they have screwed out of their benefits," I admitted.

"Let's face it, you really don't look or act like you had a stroke," Sildman said.

"I know but how about the way I feel, what I go through every day," I asked.

"I believe you, but's it will be impossible to convince the Jury," Sildman states.

"Maybe if I walked with a limp and slurred my words, is that it," I replied in disgust.

"Don't get all riled up, just go with the flow and we'll be fine. You're doing a great job showing that you are calm and level-headed. Keep it up," Sildman explained.

Sharply at 1:00, the bailiff announced, "All Rise, the Court is now in session."

I walked up to the witness stand and took my seat as Cornell approached.

The Judge addressed the Court, "I have found no precedent which would disallow this line of questioning; therefore, I will permit the Defense to continue."

"Thank you, Your Honor. Mr. Lindstrom, I just have a few more questions about your most recent employment. Once again you can start with the company name, the location where you worked and a brief description of your job duties," he instructed me.

"Sure, for the past 10 years, starting in 2008 I was employed by a Life Insurance Company in New Jersey. My job was an IT Asset Manager which means that I was responsible for tracking all computer equipment like PC's printers, servers, network and telephone equipment. I was also responsible for the financial analysis" I said.

"Did that involve a lot of detailed work with spreadsheets and the like," Cornell asked.

"Yes, it did," I replied.

"Mr. Lindstrom, you look like you're in good shape. I would bet that you could do your job again," he asked.

"Objection, your Honor! The defense cannot make observations about my client's condition," Sildman responded rather loudly.

"Sustained," said the Judge.

"I apologize, Your Honor. Mr. Lindstrom, do you think you could do your old job again," he asked.

"No Sir," I said firmly.

"May I ask why not," Cornell inquired.

"Yes, in addition to the double vision, I also have issues with severe fatigue and comprehension," I stated.

"Could you give the court some examples of you fatigue because many of the people in this courtroom are fatigued," he asked. (chuckles are heard throughout the Courtroom).

"Not like this, Sir I have to lay down and sleep every three hours. I could fall asleep sitting up," I informed him.

"Did you ever report this to your doctor," Cornell questioned.

"Yes, I reported it to every doctor I've seen," I stated.

"Isn't it true Mr. Lindstrom that this was not contained in your doctor's report of July 12, 2020, which is labeled as Exhibit D14," Cornell asked.

"I have no control over what the doctor writes. Although, this was the first topic that I discussed with him on the date you referred to" I replied vehemently.

"Can you tell the Court about your comprehension issues," he asked.

"Well, I have problems with depth perception and cannot judge distances properly. I also have to read things two to three times before I can comprehend them. I also seem to substitute words for words I thought I saw," I answered.

"I'm sorry Mr. Lindstrom," Cornell says.

"Mr. Lindstrom, do you watch television or work on the computer," he asked.

"Yes, I do," I replied.

"No more questions Your Honor," he stated as he retired to the Defense table.

"If there are no further questions, the witness is dismissed. You may step down and return to your seat," said the Judge.

"Thank you, Your Honor," I said.

Sildman announced, "Your Honor, I would like to call Dr. Ira Rosenberger as my next witness."

The doctor approached the witness stand, raises his right hand and takes the oath.

"Doctor, for the record, can you state your name and location of your practice," he asked.

Yes, my name is Dr. Ira Rosenberger. I am a partner in Neurological Partners practices in Morris Plains New Jersey," he stated.

"Thank you, Doctor. Can you also tell us what professional certifications you have earned?" Sildman inquires.

"Yes, I am a fellow of the FAACP, Doctor of Medicine from Yale and Neurological Board," the Doctor replied.

"Doctor, do you perform surgeries," Sildman asks.

"Yes, I primarily perform brain surgeries and conduct office visits for patients," Rosenberger replies.

"May I ask how long you've been in practice?"

"For 35 years," the doctor responded.

"Doctor, did you examine Mr. Lindstrom on November 20th, 2018," he inquired.

"Yes, I met with Mr. Lindstrom for the first time on November 20th 2018. I conducted an examination and I also reviewed Mr. Lindstrom's MRI results," the Doctor replied.

"Was there anyone else accompanying Mr. Lindstrom on that visit," Sildman asked.

"Yes, according to my notes, his wife was also with him and present during the examination," the doctor informed him.

"Have you ever seen a case like his before," he asked.

"Yes, I have," the doctor replied.

"Do people who have this type of brain injury ever recover," he asked.

"Some do and some don't," Rosenberger responded.

"How would you rate Mr. Lindstrom's episode," Sildman asks.

"I don't understand the question. I am not in the position to rate strokes," he stated.

"I'm sorry, did Mr. Lindstrom have a severe or mild stroke," Sildman asked.

"There is no such thing as a mild stroke. It is an injury to the brain where there is bleeding and part of the brain dies. That determines the extent, to which the stroke injury affects the physical aspects of the individual and a wide-ranging variety of motor functions," Rosenberger responded.

"Thank you, Doctor. What were your findings after examining Mr. Lindstrom," he asked.

"According to the MRI, which was on a DVD, showed an infarction of the thalamus, both left and right side. The thalamus is basically a relay to the brain's cortex. A switching station so to speak. It relays messages from our sensory preceptors which instruct the brain how to process the request," the doctor stated.

"Doesn't the blood just dry up in there and put everything back to normal," Sildman inquired.

"I wish it were that easy and then I wouldn't have a job and people wouldn't suffer. To answer your question directly, the interrupted blood flow starves the brain and a s result, part of the brain can no longer function. Mr. Lindstrom complains of double vision, severe fatigue and comprehension issues," he stated.

"Have you seen these types of issues with patients who have had similar brain injuries as Mr. Lindstrom's?" Sildman asked.

"Yes, absolutely. All of these complaints are completely consistent with the type of episode Mr. Lindstrom experienced. There were no anomalies" the Doctor states.

"Doctor, one last question if I may? Mr. Lindstrom looks just fine to me, could he be faking his symptoms," he asked.

"I am asked this question quite often especially from insurance companies. Unfortunately, when we think of stroke victims, they exhibit physical symptoms such as paralysis on one side of the body and slurred speech. Those types of strokes, which are the majority of strokes, are typically caused by a blood clot which travels to the brain and result in a massive impact. These are known technically as atrial fibrillizations or "afib" in short. Mr. Lindstrom's injury was caused by a rupture in blood vessels which caused a bleed in the brain. I think I have already described this," he stated.

"You did, Doctor. Thank you, Doctor. No further questions," Sildman stated.

I really didn't care for the doctor when I met with him, but I was really impressed by his testimony. Now to see if the Defense can tear him apart.

Defense attorney David Rosen arose and approached the witness stand.

"Good Afternoon, Dr. Rosenberger" as Rosen greeted the doctor.

"Good Afternoon," the Doctor replied.

"How would you characterize Mr. Lindstrom's progress since the time you saw him in November of 2018," Rosen asked.

"I do not measure progress. That is up to the patient or rehabilitation. My practice is limited to diagnosis and surgery" Rosenberger responded.

"So, you have no way of telling if Mr. Lindstrom has improved enough to return to work," he inquired.

"Objection, Your Honor. We've already addressed this issue," Sildman stated.

"Sustained," said the Judge.

"Ok then Doctor, you have only seen Mr. Lindstrom once, is that correct," he asked.

"Yes," said the doctor.

"And what did you tell him after you examined him?" Rosen questioned.

"I advised him that I thought his condition had plateaued and that he may or may not see improvements. I also told him that he should call me immediately if his symptoms should change," he said.

"Has Mr. Lindstrom called you since his original appointment two years ago," he asked.

"Not that I am aware of" the doctor replies.

"Doctor, do you complete questionnaires from insurance companies advising them of your findings following an examination," he questioned.

"Yes, I do," the doctor replied.

"Are you ever asked in these questionnaires if you patient can perform certain tasks," he asked.

"Yes, I do see these types of questions," he stated.

"How did you respond to Mr. Lindstrom's questionnaire," he asked.

"I'm sorry but I do not recall," he replied.

"Let me take a moment to refresh your memory Doctor. I am reading from Exhibit D17, dated December 27, 2020 and signed by Dr. Rosenberger," he said.

He handed the document to the Doctor.

"Sir, it that your signature," he asked.

"Yes, it is," Rosenberger responded.

"Let me read a few questions from this questionnaire along with your responses. Question #1 on the survey, in your professional opinion, do you believe that the patient could perform the operational demands of his current occupation? Your response, no due to issues with diplopia," he quoted.

"Is it true that Mr. Lindstrom has corrective glasses for diplopia which is also known as double vision," he asked.

"Yes, I believe he does," he replied.

"Ok, onto Question #2: if the answer to Question #1 is No, would Mr. Lindstrom have the ability to perform, lighter occupational demands such as lifting less than 10lbs. sitting and occasionally standing, planning the activity of others, making judgements and decisions, dealing with people? Your answer Doctor was yes. Is that correct," he inquired.

"I believe so," he stated.

"Thank you, Doctor. No further questions," he informed us.

The Judge announced, "The Jury will recess for the day and return here tomorrow at 8:00 a.m. sharp. No delays and no excuses. Let me also remind the Jury that you are not permitted to discuss the case with anyone and that includes your family. Also, newspaper reporters and television station may ask you to comment on these proceedings. "No Comment" is the appropriate answer. Are there any questions," he asked.

Grumblings of "no" were heard from the Jury box

"Ok then, enjoy your evening," the Judge declared.

The Judge bangs his gavel on his bench.

As the courtroom empties out, my wife approaches me and my lawyer. "I can't stand it anymore" she announced. How are we doing Mr. Sildman?"

"I didn't like the Doctor much but he did a great job at strengthening our case, but the real fireworks will start tomorrow when we hear from the insurance company employees. I don't expect to get much from them except for the corporate bullshit," stated Sildman.

"My concern is when they present the CEO and Managers of the Insurance company. They have been rehearsing for weeks and months and can be pretty convincing. Remember, that they have been through this before and they have always won, except for once I believe in a class action suit. There is no need to worry. Go have a nice dinner and make sure you get plenty of rest. These trials can wear you out," my attorney suggested.

My wife and I walked to the parking lot to retrieve our car. It was a short walk and my wife lovingly said "how are you feeling?" She was obviously concerned about my health and remarks like these always confirmed she was the one to marry.

"I'm not really sure" I said. "Thought we were doing really well, but Sildman keeps bringing me down," I continued.

"My wife said "I don't think he's doing it on purpose, but rather to manage your expectations if you should lose." Once again, she always had my back.

"I can't lose" I said. "I have too many other people depending on a positive outcome," I explained.

She said "I know Dear, but you a carrying a huge burden that isn't yours."

"Really, then who does it belong to? I'm sorry, that wasn't right, I apologize," I quickly added.

"No need to, Bill" she replied. God, I love this girl!

We finally got into the car. "OK if we eat at the hotel tonight," I asked her.

"Sure, that's fine. Let's see what type of menu they have" she replied.

On most other nights I would have found a fancy restaurant where we could get a steak, but tonight I was not up to it. It didn't take long to get to the hotel. My wife didn't say a word the whole trip. I kept thinking about tomorrow. This wasn't really fair to her but she did ask to come along.

We dropped off the car for valet parking and entered the lobby which was very beautiful. At the Check-In Counter, they asked if I would like a "city view".

"Yes, of course" I responded.

Our room was on the 18th floor. I wanted to head straight for the bar but my wife commandeered me to the elevator and then to our room. Our room was very nice and had a terrific view of the city. In fact, it was very romantic. But romance was failing me because of ED. You know, the condition where you just can't get it up no matter how hard you try. I understand the physiological aspects of it, but I don't like it. I also don't think that women understand how important this is to a man. Anyway, I'll take a shower, get changed and go down for dinner. My wife changed and she looked great! Now it's my turn and although I tried to dress up, I really didn't feel like myself. Some wine will fix that!

We took the elevator down to the lobby and then to the restaurant. I prepared to be disappointed. Actually, the restaurant was very nice with candle lit tables and booths.

The waiter approached and said "Welcome to the Elegance Ristorante, my name is Paul and I will be serving you this evening. May we start with a cocktail?"

"Yes, I'll have a glass of Chardonnay," I answered.

"Madam," he inquired.

"I will have glass of Pinot Noir, thank you," my wife replied.

What the hell is wrong with me, the lady is always served first. I ordered the lamb chops and my wife ordered a salad. For the life of me, I will never understand why she always ordered lettuce whenever we dine out.

We didn't say much during dinner although my wife tried to engage me in conversation. Unfortunately, my thoughts were on the pending events of tomorrow.

"Why don't you just let it go," she asked pleasantly.

"Mary, I can't, I wish I could," I admitted sheepishly.

"Ok, let's talk about the kids," as she suggested to change the subject.

"Oh, the ones who couldn't come because their lives are too important," I reminded her.

"No, the ones who love you dearly and have family obligations," she corrected me.

Ok, I just got a whoopin' and I need to settle down, I supposed.

"I'm sorry, it seems that's all I say these days is 'I'm sorry,' This thing is consuming me," I apologize.

"Yes, because you let it," she said.

Holy shit, she's right, I thought. If we lose the monthly disability income, so what? We won't starve, we won't be on the streets and we will have the income from that book you are writing especially when it gets on the Best Sellers list. I thought to myself.

"May I interest you in desert and coffee or tea," the hunk of a waiter asked.

"Yes, I'll have cherry cheesecake," I said.

There I go again, putting myself before my wife.

"I'm sorry, my wife should order first" I said sheepishly.

"I'll just have Green Tea please," my weight conscious wife requested.

"Thank you, Madam" Paul replied politely.

"See there I go again, I'm Sorry," I told her.

"Don't be silly, you've always been like that. It really doesn't bother me," she told me.

We didn't speak much during dessert. "Ready," I asked.

"Yes, I'm tired," she replied.

We walked slowly to the elevator and returned to the lavish room. As my wife changed for bed, I looked out over the city and kind of questioned how I got here. Nonetheless, I'm knee deep in it now and I've got to follow it through. Mary came in, turned on the news and got into bed. I took off my clothes and went into the bathroom. By the time I returned, she was dead asleep. I guess I should be lucky for having such an understanding wife since I am a shit. I turned the light out and rolled over gingerly so as not to wake her up. After all, she's doing this for us!

The Trial - Day Two

The next morning the alarm went off at 5:30 a.m., but the room was still pitch black. I wasn't used to getting up so early but my wife has to take a shower and do the womanly prep. I decided I'd just roll around in bed until the absolute last minute. I must have drifted off again because I heard her say, "Your turn."

I could have stayed in this shower forever and never worry about hot water. Today I am wearing a blue suit, white shirt and a red tie. Very professional look if I do say so myself. I was clean shaven with flowing white hair neatly combed. Damn, I look good. Just like in Corporate America. My shoes are shined and I looked to make sure my belt is on, all ready to go. Mary even said "You look very handsome, my love."

I keep remembering what my lawyer said, "Not too flashy." Everyone will be looking at you especially the jury." I must admit that my wife looked pretty damn good as well. You get used to seeing joggers everyday but when she's dressed, she looks like a million bucks. I'm so very glad she was the one I proposed to! I was a damn lucky guy!

It was a short drive from the hotel to the courthouse. We got prime parking again and quickly entered the courthouse. I thought it would have been a good day for a walk. As we entered, I noticed people looking at us. Mary took her seat and I proceeded to the plaintiff's table. My lawyer was already there and today he had on a conservative gray suit.

"Good Morning Bill," he addressed me.

"Good Morning Mitch," I responded.

"How was your evening," Mitch asked.

"Nice" I responded. I am obviously not one for conversation in the morning. I'm not a morning person you could say.

"Well, today will be interesting to say the least. They will skewer our witness and then they will turn up the heat to completely discredit you. Remember, calm and cool-headed. They will say things that want to make you jump up and punch them out but it's all tactical. It's a game. A hellish game and sometimes, I really wonder about it. Anyway, good luck.

Things are looking good for us so far and they know it," Mitch assured me.

"Have they approached you about a settlement yet," I asked.

"No, and I don't expect them to. They are too good at this," he retorted.

At this point, the jury filed into the courtroom and took their seats, the same seats as yesterday.

The Bailiff announces "Ladies and Gentleman, please rise. The Honorable Douglas Bradford presiding. Please be seated."

The judge addressed the jury; "Ladies and Gentlemen, I trust you had a good evening and I want to personally thank you for your service in the Judicial system. The role you are playing is extremely important and one of the basic tenants that this great country is built upon. As a reminder, in this case we have the Plaintiff, Mr. Lindstrom who has accused the Pluriman Insurance Company of violating the Employee Retirement Income Security Act of 1974. Mr. Lindstrom is asking to have his disability payments restored. Please be aware that each party is required to supply evidence to support their position. Therefore, as we continue this case, please keep this in mind. Mr. Sildman, are you prepared to call your next witness?"

"Yes, Your Honor, I am. The Plaintiff would like to call Mrs. Mildred Brown," he requested.

As I watched her walk toward the witness stand, she looked to be in her 50's with short brown hair and on the heavy side. She has dressed nicely with a blue flowered dress.

"Do you swear to tell the truth, the whole truth and nothing but the truth," the Bailiff asked.

"I Do," she responded firmly.

My lawyer approached the stand.

"Good morning, Mrs. Brown," he addressed.

"Good Morning," she replied.

"Is it true that you worked for the Pluriman Insurance Company," he asked.

"Yes Sir, that's true," she admitted.

"Mrs. Brown could you tell the court how long you worked for the Pluriman Insurance Company and your title," he requested.

"Yes, I worked for Pluriman for 22 years and my title was Senior Client Services Representative" she responded.

"Mrs. Brown, could you describe you job duties and responsibilities for the court," asked Sildman.

"Yes Sir, I was assigned disability clients and I was the primary contact for any questions or issues for the client. I would also send questionnaires to the clients' doctors following their doctor's appointments. I also scheduled doctor's appointments for clients as requested by the Pluriman medical staff. Is that good enough," she asked.

"Yes, thank you, Mrs. Brown," he answered.

"May I ask how frequently you would be paid for your services," was the next question.

"I was paid bi-weekly, twice a month and then would get a bonus on a quarterly basis," she replied.

"A bonus for working?" Sildman asked confusedly.

"No Sir, the bonus had to be earned," she replied.

"I'm sorry, Mrs. Brown, could you clarify how you earned a bonus," Sildman inquired.

"Yes Sir, the bonus amount was based on the percentage of money I saved the company by getting people off of disability," she replied unsure she should say that!

"Objection, Your Honor. The plaintiff's statements are not accurate. Employees are not required to get people off of disability as Mrs. Brown suggests," he excitedly replies.

"Sustained," the judge called out.

"Mrs. Brown, could you describe in more detail the process by which an individual would have their disability payments discontinued," Sildman asked.

Wow, my lawyer was good. I saw exactly what he was doing. He is baiting them so they can cross-exam her. Brilliant, I thought.

"I would be given the names of individuals who would be under investigation. I would then begin looking for opportunities to show that the individual had violated the contract with Pluriman," Mildred replied.

"Objection, Your Honor. Once again misleading statements by the witness. It was not Mrs. Brown's job to evaluate contracts," Rosen stated.

"Sustained," said the Judge.

"Mrs. Brown, could you re-phrase your answer please," Sildman requested.

"I'll try. I would review the computer records of the individual and see if there was anything unusual," she convinced him.

"Can you give the Court some examples," he asked.

"Yes, I'd look to see if someone has missed a doctor's appointment or if a doctor responded positively to our questionnaire. I would check to see if the individual was working without notifying us. I would also make recommendations if I thought that the individual was qualified to return to work. Is that good enough?" she asked.

"Yes, Ma'am, thank you," he replied.

"You're welcome," Mildred replied unsure of herself.

"Mrs. Brown, I am still confused about this bonus payment. You said that you were paid a portion of the savings if the disability payment was discontinued. How did you discontinue payments," Sildman asked coyishly?

"Typically, we would send the client a letter indicating what part of the contract was in violation and would drop the person within 30 days" she replied.

"Did you make that decision," he inquired.

"No, no, I would send my findings to my supervisor, a consultant assigned to our department and my contact in the law department. They would actually make the decision and let me know the exact wording I should use to respond to the client. I would then prepare a letter and send it back to them for review," she explained.

"How long typically did that process take," Sildman inquired.

"Usually under three days, I believe" Mildred replied.

"Mrs. Brown, assuming that a client had violated the contract and was dropped by the company, how would your bonus be paid? If you could give an example that would be great," he asked.

"Ok, let's say a client was on disability for five years and at the end of year two, the client violated the contract. There would be three years of payments that the company did not have to pay, so I would get a percentage of the total outstanding payment amount," she explained.

"Do you remember what the percentage was," Sildman asked.

"As I recall it was somewhere around five or six percent," she replied.

"Wow that's a great percentage. May I ask, in 22 years how many times you missed getting a bonus," he continued his questioning.

"Never," she adamantly stated.

"When was the last time you worked for Pluriman, Mrs. Brown," he asked.

"Approximately 2 years ago" she said.

"So, the information you are providing to the court is relatively current," he asked.

"Objection, Your Honor. There is no basis for establishing currency. Our policies and practices are continually changing. The job Mrs. Brown performed two years ago may be a completely different job today," David Rosen stated.

"Sustained," said the Judge.

"Mrs. Brown did you ever discontinue disability benefits for any client you thought should be on continued disability," he asked.

"Yes," she said.

"Objection Your Honor. The question is a matter of opinion not supported by fact. May I ask, Your Honor that the plaintiff's counsel be reprimanded for this continued line of questioning," Rosen asked.

"Sustained and I will not be told when to reprimand attorneys, thank you" the Judge answered angrily.

"Mr. Sildman, you have many years of experience and you should know better. I take it that you have never appeared in my courtroom before, but I will not tolerate this type of questioning. I would ask that the last question and response be stricken from the record and the jury is to disregard it," he continued.

"I'm very sorry, Your Honor. It will not happen again," said Mr. Sildman apologetically.

"Mrs. Brown, over your 22 years career at Pluriman, how many letters have you sent to clients to deny disability benefits," Sildman asked.

"I'm not really sure of an exact number but it would be well over 1,000," she replied.

"No further questions Your Honor" he stated as he walked. back to his seat.

"The court will recess for 15 minutes. Please be back in your seats by 10:30 and no discussions," as the Judge ordered everyone in the courtroom.

My lawyer was speaking to Mrs. Brown for a few minutes and then returned to the table.

"How are we doing," I asked once more.

"Mrs. Brown did great, but wait until they get ahold of her. She's a pretty tough cookie so I'm not that worried. She is also a very credible witness with 22 years of experience. That's exactly what I wanted. It will be difficult for them to pull one over on her," he informed me.

The jury and the courtroom observers made their way back slowly but surely into the courtroom on time. I glanced around and saw Mary and gave her a wink.

"All come to Order," The bailiff commanded.

"The Defense may now question the witness. I will remind you that you are still under oath. Proceed, Counselor" the judge directed David Rosen.

"Thank You, Your Honor," Rosen replied.

Good Morning, Mrs. Brown, my name is David Rosen and I am the Lead Defense Lawyer for your old employer, Pluriman Insurance Company. Mrs. Brown, in your earlier testimony you stated that you had been employed by Pluriman for 22 years," Rosen stated.

"That's correct" she said emphatically.

"Under what conditions did you leave the company two years ago," he questioned.

"I'm not sure I understand the question," she replied.

"I'm sorry, let me clarify, did you just quit? Did you retire? Did you find another job? Did you hit the lottery," he asked sarcastically. (courtroom chuckles could be heard).

"I was terminated," Mildred admitted.

"Ouch, I bet that hurt after 22 years," Rosen questioned.

No comment from Mrs. Brown was heard.

"Mrs. Brown, can you tell the court what the reason was for your termination," Rosen asked.

"Yes, I was not getting enough disability clients off the ranks," she said forcefully.

"I suppose that was written up in your performance review?" Rosen questioned.

"Objection, Your Honor. Counsel is leading the witness," Sildman interjected.

"Sustained," said the Judge.

"Ok, Mrs. Brown, do you remember when your last performance review was," asked Rosen.

"Not exactly but I think it was a few months before they let me go," she retorted matter of factly.

"Mrs. Brown, I submit to the court Exhibit D22 which is dated November 21, 2018. If I may Your Honor, I would like to read a passage from that review," Rosen requested.

"Proceed Counselor," the Judge instructed.

"Mildred has not been performing up to expectations. She has continually been behind in her objectives that are required for a Senior Client Services Representative. We have received numerous complaints from her Clients which have been documented and discussed with her. We are hopeful that her performance improves and we will be continually monitoring her progress and will assist in any way that we can," he read off the paper.

"Mrs. Brown, does this sound familiar," Rosen questioned.

"Yes, it does," she replied.

"I don't see anywhere that there is a reference to the number of clients for which you discontinued disability. Mrs. Brown, May I ask who conducted your Performance Review," he inquired.

"Yes, it was Matthew Whitman, my Manager at the time," she admitted.

"Thank You." Mrs. Brown, is it true that you suffer from depression," he asked her.

"Objection," Sildman exclaims. "Relevance," he asked.

"Overruled," the Judge exclaimed.

"Yes, I do," Mildred answered.

"How long have you had this condition," Rosen asks.

"Most of my life," she replied.

"Do you take medication for this condition," he interrogated.

"Yes, I do," she informed him.

"Mrs. Brown, do you think your condition affected your performance at Pluriman Insurance," he asked

"No, I do not. My condition is controlled by medication," she replied.

"Then why did your performance decline? Were you having issues with depression," Rosen questioned.

"Objection, Your Honor," Sildman stated emphatically.

"Sustained," the judge responded.

"May I answer the question, Your Honor," Mildred asked the judge.

"Yes, please, go ahead Mrs. Brown," he stated.

"The company was always increasing the number of clients they wanted to get off of disability, I simply couldn't keep up," she explained.

"Mrs. Brown, I don't see any reference in your performance review to the number of clients you were required to get off disability. Where did this number come from," he demanded.

"My boss. They always had targets we needed to hit and if we didn't, we would be reprimanded," she exclaimed.

"Oh, so there was nothing documented, only hearsay," he inquired.

"No, it was known throughout the company that there were targets that needed to be achieved," she told him.

"Is this documented in the Company's Policy and Procedures Manual," he continued.

"I'm not sure," she said.

"Your Honor, let me introduce, Exhibit D11 which is the Pluriman Insurance Company, Policy and Procedures Manual for client services representatives. Upon examination Your Honor, you will see that there is absolutely no reference to discontinuing disability coverage or target established for Client Services Representatives. So, Mrs. Brown, if I may summarize, you were terminated in February 2019 for not hitting your targets and those targets were not documented in your performance review before you were terminated. In addition, you signed this review which acknowledged your agreement. Correct," Rosen asked.

"Yes," she replied.

"Mrs. Brown, was your employer, Pluriman Insurance aware of your condition," he asked.

"Objection, Your Honor. The witness cannot comment on what her employer knew or didn't know," Sildman stated.

"Sustained," the Judge replied.

"Mrs. Brown have you ever seen a psychiatrist," he asked.

"Objection, Your Honor, relevancy," Sildman questioned.

"Sustained," the Judge replied.

"Mrs. Brown, in the course of your work, did you have access to the Company's Policy and Procedures Manual," Rosen asked.

"Yes, I did," she replied.

"Can you tell me if that at any time in the 22 years with the company did the manual or any revisions contain any information about quotas, targets or verbiage about getting to get clients off of disability?"

"I'm not sure, it's been a long time," she answered.

"Mrs. Brown, did the targets and quotas that you testified about ever change," Rosen asked.

"Yes, they would be different every quarter," she informed him.

"And how did you receive those numbers? Were they emailed to you or verbally communicated," he asked.

"They were always verbally communicated to me by my boss," she explained.

"What would happen to an employee if they didn't hit their targets," Rosen asked.

"Objection Your Honor. The witness cannot testify to discussions that other employees had with their Manager," Sildman stated.

"Sustained," the Judge replied.

"Mrs. Brown, what would your manager say to you if you didn't achieve your target," he inquired.

"He would usually say that he was disappointed and that I needed to try harder because he didn't want to make it into a performance issue. It was usually a pleasant conversation," she stated.

Sildman whispered to me, "Damn it, she shouldn't have said that. We talked about this. Don't add anything extra that you're not asked about."

"Mrs. Brown, couldn't you work on just the clients that had the highest percentage of payout for your bonus," asked Rosen.

"No, I was given the priority and sequence of client issues that I needed to address," she said.

"And who would provide you with that information Mrs. Brown," he asked.

"My boss would and he would get it from a consultant," she replied.

"Damn it, she just did it again," Sildman whispered.

"Mrs. Brown, did the company call these quarterly payout "bonuses," he inquired.

"No, I can't remember the exact term but we all called them bonuses," she explained.

"I believe that the company refers to these as "incentive compensation," stated Rosen.

"Yes, that's the word," she replied.

"May I ask what you would do with the money that you would receive," he asked her.

"Objection, Your Honor, not relevant," Sildman stated.

"Sustained," the Judge said.

"So, you worked for the company for 22 years, you must have thought these bonuses were a good thing," he asked.

"Objection, leading the witness," Sildman called out.

"Sustained," replied the Judge.

"Mrs. Brown, I assumed you cashed all of your bonus checks and didn't reject any of the payments, is that correct," he questioned.

"Yes Sir," she answered.

"Did you ever tell the company that you could not accept the payment because it was unethical," he asked sarcastically.

"No Sir," she replied.

"Mrs. Brown did you ever communicate to the company in any way in regard to the bonus," he asked.

"No Sir," she retorted indignantly.

"So, I assume you were pretty satisfied with the whole process," he asked.

"Objection," Sildman exclaimed.

"Sustained," the judge says wearily. He was clearly growing tired of the objections.

"Just a few more questions, Mrs. Brown and we'll let you go. Do you have any ill will or feel any animosity toward the Pluriman Insurance Company," he asked of her.

"Beside the fact that they terminated me without a valid cause," she asked.

"Damn it, that was a trap and she fell right into it. She just showed that she does harbor bad feelings about the company." Sildman whispered to me. "Watch out for those traps," he directed.

"No further questions, Your Honor," he finished.

"Thank you, Counselor. Mrs. Brown, you are excused. At this point we will break for lunch and I would ask everyone to be in their seats by 1:30 p.m.," the judge requested.

As Mildred passed our table my lawyer smiled at her sheepishly.

"Aren't you going to tell her that she screwed us, I asked my lawyer.

"No, it's too late now. Nothing we can do about it. I will just need to tear into her manager who is the next witness on tap. These guys will lie their asses off to protect their jobs and the company. Wait until you see this circus," he promised.

"We're going to lose, aren't we," I asked disappointedly.

"Would you please stop? This is the way trials go. There are ups and downs, wins and losses but in the end the jury decides and that's who we are playing to. I know it's difficult to understand, but I have been doing this my whole life. Just relax and enjoy the show," he explained.

I thought he must have some degree of confidence if he's telling me to relax. My wife had been standing behind us patiently waiting for me to go to lunch.

"I'm sorry Dear, just wanted to get a read on things. Let's grab a sandwich," I suggested.

Sildman reached into his bag and pulled out a brown bag and newspaper. He nodded congenially at my wife. What was he up to?

We left the courthouse and went to a little lunch place next door to the courthouse. The place was packed but they were moving fast. As we stood in line, I looked at the lunch board menu and thought about a giant roast beef hoagie, but instead opted for a tuna on rye. My wife, of course, ordered a salad. Some things never change.

As I glanced around, I couldn't help but notice some of the jurors were seated there. I had been looking at them for two days now. They were all laughing and seemed like they were in a good mood. I didn't notice them looking at me but they may have been when I was turned the other way. I'm sure the guys were looking at my wife because she looked hot today.

We grabbed our lunch to go and went to the local park which is just outside the courthouse. After all, I don't want to be late. That would leave a lasting impression on the judge and jury.

As we started to eat, I asked my wife "How do you think it's going from where you sit?"

"I think it's going Ok, but I really can't stand those defense lawyers. They're obnoxious," she answered.

"I can't either, but my lawyer says they're doing the best they can to discredit the witness. Wow this is really good tuna, how's your salad," I inquired.

"Good" my wife replies.

I thought to myself how many different variations of lettuce are there?

"After lunch we will hear from Mildred Brown's manager. My lawyer says they lie through their teeth. Should be interesting. He also says that the trial is moving along quickly so the judge isn't getting annoyed," I told her.

"I guess that's good news," she said.

"Let's finish up so we can get back," I said.

"Ok, but we have plenty of time," she explained.

"But I need to go to the Men's room and you know how long that can take," I told her.

"I figured as much," she said.

When we returned to the courtroom, it was relatively empty. The guard gave me a strange look when I went in. I wondered what that meant. Slowly the courtroom started to fill up. I was looking around to see if I could spot Mildred Brown's manager. I've never seen him before, but I'm sure I can spot a corporate liar. As everyone is seated, I noticed that the Judge was late. Suddenly the bailiff announces, "All rise, the Honorable Douglas Bradford presiding. All come to order. Please be seated."

"Mr. Rosen, would you call your next witness please," the judge asks.

"Yes, Your Honor. The Defense calls Mr. Steven Whitman," he called out.

As he arose, I notice that he had the requisite corporate attire. I should know, since I used to wear it myself. He was tall, handsome, in his late forties and clean-cut. Couldn't help but notice his shiny shoes. Spit polished all the way. Not a sign of gray in his brown hair. He probably dyes it. Corporate asshole I decided.

"Mr. Whitman, do you swear to tell the truth, the whole truth and nothing but the truth so help you God," the bailiff asked.

"I do," Whitman replied.

Lyin' piece of shit, I thought.

"Mr. Whitman, could you tell the court your title and the number of years you've been employed by the Pluriman Insurance Company," Rosen asks.

"Yes Sir, my name is Matthew Whitman and my title is senior manager of client services. I have been with Pluriman Insurance for 10 years," he explained.

"And before Pluriman did you hold similar positions?" Rosen asks.

"Yes Sir, prior to Pluriman I worked for National Insurance for 20 years," he informed us.

"Mr. Whitman, why did you leave National," he inquired.

"Pluriman made me an offer I couldn't refuse," he stated. (There is laughter in the Courtroom).

Asshole, I was thinking.

"Mr. Whitman, is it true that you personally supervised Mrs. Mildred Brown for the last five years of her career with Pluriman," Rosen inquires.

"Yes, that's correct," Whitman responded.

"Can you tell us a little bit about Mrs. Brown's performance while she worked for you," he asked.

"Mildred was a great person. She was a hard worker, pleasant personality, easy to get along with and her Client's loved her. She would always meet her objectives up until the last year of her employment. I noticed that her work started to decline and she wasn't meeting her work objectives. We also started to get complaints about her from Clients which was very unusual," Whitman replied.

"Mr. Whitman, did you have any conversations with Mrs. Brown about these issues," he inquired.

"Yes, we had several discussions during the year," he said confidently.

"Did you document these discussions," Rosen asked.

"No, I really didn't see the need, I figured that she was just in a slump. It happens sometimes and I find that it is best to work with the employee to help them get back in the game," Whitman replied.

Bullshit you lying bastard I said under my breath.

"Mr. Whitman, isn't it true that you did document these issues in her Performance Review dated November 21, 2018. Also known to the court as Exhibit D22," Rosen stated.

"Unfortunately, yes. I had tried everything, I suggested outside counseling, self-improvement courses an even a motivational seminar. I thought that I had given it enough time. I worked closely with our Human Resources Department to rectify the situation. I was reaching out to get all the help I could because Mrs. Brown was a very valuable employee to our company. Our Human Resources thought that as a last resort, we should write up the issues in her Performance Review as a way of snapping her out of it. I wish things didn't have to come to that. The Pluriman Insurance Company places great value on our people and we do whatever we can to help them. It's the company policy" Whitman retorts.

"Thank You Mr. Whitman" Rosen said.

"Another question. In Mrs. Brown's testimony she stated that you would supply he with quotas or targets for getting client's off of disability. Is that true," inquires Rosen.

"No, but I think this needs some explanation. May I continue," asked Whitman.

Here it comes, he's going to lay it on thick. Let me get my boots on for the bullshit he is about to spew. How do these guys look themselves in the mirror every day? What do they tell their wives and family about how they screw the employee? There should be a check box on the Employment Application that says. "Do you have skills in lying to employees. Please check Yes or No.

Whitman starts to speak again, "We, I mean all of us at Pluriman Insurance, strive to do the utmost for our Client's that have suffered disabling injuries, by providing a safety net of continued income. Most employers carry this type of insurance as a benefit for their employees. We truly hope that employees never have to use our services, but in life, bad things happen to good people. We provide monthly cash payments to our clients and in turn, all we ask is that they adhere to the terms of the contractual agreement that we sign with them" Whitman stated.

"What is this agreement and when do clients sign it?" Rosen inquired.

"Usually following an accident or a hospitalization, an employee would send their medical records to our company.

We have a number of Doctors and specialists on staff who review these records and make determination's about disability payments. I, or my staff, never make these types of decisions. They are made by experts and often require technical medical data. Typically, a person is granted Short Term disability and if often followed by Long Term disability. We do everything in our power to do what's right for the client. Once a client is approved, then they are assigned to my group and I, in turn, assign a client services representative. This person is assigned permanently so we don't move people around. Clients have one and only one single point of contact throughout their disability."

"Your Honor, I would like to identify Exhibit D5 which is the Pluriman contract that is supplied to everyone that applies for disability" Rosen requested.

"So noted," said the Judge.

"Mr. Whitman, this contract is rather large, could you summarize the client's responsibilities in this contract," Rosen asked.

"Objection, Your Honor, the witness is not an attorney nor does he have the qualifications for interpreting contractual law" Sildman called out.

"Overruled. The gentleman is providing a summary and is under oath to tell the truth," the Judge stated.

"Thank you, Your Honor. Mr. Whitman could you please supply the Court with a truthful summary of the client's obligations under this contact?" Rosen asked the witness.

"Yes Sir, I will," Whitman replies firmly.

"And Mr. Whitman please use laymen's terms and no technical jargon" Rosen requested.

"I will sir. Ok, the agreement states a number of things that the client must do while they are receiving disability payments. First, they must notify Pluriman in any changes in their medical condition, good or bad. The client must notify Pluriman of all doctors' appointments even if they are not related to the persons condition or illness. On occasion, we will ask clients to attend medical examinations so we can better understand their condition and determine if they require additional help. We make all of the arrangements and will supply transportation to and from the doctor. I think that's pretty great" Whitman stated.

"No side comments please sir" as the Judge admonished the witness.

"I'm sorry, Your Honor. We also ask that clients notify us in writing of any changes in employment status. In other words, if a client has been laid off or has gotten another job. We pay clients benefits due to lost wages and if they should get another job, they would no longer collect disability. We refer to this as double-dipping," Whitman responded.

"That sounds relatively straight forward," Rosen stated.

"We do encourage clients to take this document to an attorney of their choice so they can understand all of the aspects of the contract before signing it," Whitman advised.

Mr. Whitman, speaking of attorneys, I was curious about how many attorneys do you have working at your company," Rosen asked.

"I'm not sure of the exact number but I would venture to say that it's in the hundreds. In addition, we have independent attorneys that are consultants and we also go to outside firms for advice and guidance," Whitman replied.

"And what exactly do all of these attorneys do," Rosen inquired.

"Well, the medical field has a lot of different specialties, the attorneys are also specialized. Everything that we do is reviewed by an attorney. All of the correspondence from clients is reviewed by an attorney and all of the correspondence we send to a Client is reviewed by an attorney. Compliance with the law is always in the forefront of our business," Whitman stated.

"Do the attorney's set the quotas or targets," asked Rosen.

"No, no, no, let me clarify about quotas and targets. There are many times when a client is in non-compliance with our contractual agreement. Sometimes a client forgets about the detail in the agreement. Once we identify this, we contact the law department to review the particular non-compliance issue. It is up to them to determine if a client has broken the agreement and as a result, their benefits would be terminated. This is basic Contract Law and is no different than any other agreement between two parties. When this happens, we receive notification from the attorney that the benefits must be terminated. I hate to see this happen but it does unfortunately. This is where the so-called quotas or targets come from," Whitman responded.

"Mr. Whitman have there been times when you mistakenly discontinued someone's benefits and had to reinstate the benefits?" asked Rosen.

"Yes, unfortunately that does happen on a rare occasion. When this does happen, we make every effort to reimburse for lost payments and reinstate the Client in good standing."

"Mr. Whitman, did you personally terminate Mildred Brown," Rosen inquired.

"Yes, I'm sorry to say that I did, however, this occurred after exhaustive meetings with our Human Resources partners. This is not something that I am permitted to do on my own nor am I proud of it. We have a corporate responsibility to make sure she received severance pay for the many years of excellent service to our Company, as well as Outplacement Services. I believe that she also received Unemployment Compensation," Whitman said.

"So, you just didn't throw her out the door," Rosen questioned.

"No Sir, not at all. That is not how Pluriman conducts business. Although it's never a good situation for anyone, we wanted to do what we felt was right," he explained.

"Thank you, Mr. Whitman. Your witness, Mr. Sildman., Rosen stated.

The Judge began to speak, "The court will recess for the day and we will continue at 9:00 a.m. tomorrow for the cross examination by the plaintiff. The Jury knows what I am about to say, but in the interest of this case, no discussion and no speaking with third parties. Understood," he declared

"Yes, Your Honor," could be heard throughout the crowded courtroom.

My attorney looked at me and said, "I'm satisfied. That was a whole lot of corporate bullshit. I know it, you know it and the Jury knows it. That's exactly what we wanted. They think they're slick, but people see through that crap. When will they ever learn? Are we feelin' good," he boasted.

"Yes, we are," I replied.

"Go get a nice dinner for you and the Mrs.," Sildman requested.

"I will do that," I said.

The courtroom emptied out and my wife came down to the plaintiff's table.

"Hey Hon, are you in the mood for Chinese food," I asked.

"I sure am," she said excitedly.

"Ok, let's get outta here," I suggested.

We hustled down to the Parking Lot to retrieve our car and there was an illegal parking sticker on the car.

"How about we go back to the hotel, get freshened up and then go for Chinese? Remember they don't have salads there," I said jokingly.

"I know, Mr. Wise Ass," was her reply.

It was a short drive to the hotel and we made it to our room in no time.

"How much is this room costing us per night?" my wife asked.

"One hundred and seventy-five a night," I told her.

"I hope this trial is over soon before we go broke," she said.

"I think it's pretty close to the end," I assured her.

"I hope so because I'm really getting tired of the bullshit," she grumbled.

"So am I Dear. Have you ever heard so much corporate crap in your lifetime," I inquired.

"No, but isn't that what you did for a living," she asked me.

"Yeah, I guess you're right. I wonder if these guys actually believe the shit they are spewing out," I asked.

"Of course not, it's all an act. You are really upbeat today," she said.

"I don't know what it is but I do feel good and I'm starving for Chinese! Ok let's go," I demanded.

I found a restaurant close to the hotel so we decided to walk. The city seemed pretty safe, so I wasn't concerned. I called for a reservation and they said they don't take them and the wait was only a half hour because it was still early in the evening. Before we knew it, we were there. The atmosphere was very authentic and we were greeted right away.

"Table for two," the hostess asked.

"Yes please," I said.

"Right this way" as she directed us to our table.

Wow, we didn't even need to wait. Things were looking up. I already knew what I wanted, hot & sour soup, egg roll, moo-shoo pork and fortune cookie. I remember this time that my wife orders first. She orders won-ton soup, coconut shrimp and egg roll.

They didn't serve alcohol, but man could I have used some wine after the day in court.

"This is a really nice place; how did you find it," my wife asked.

"I looked through the literature at the hotel and this place was on the top of the list. The reviews said the food was excellent so I thought, let's give it a shot."

"Good choice. Great atmosphere," she added.

Before we knew it, we were served. The food was excellent and I enjoyed everything. My wife couldn't finish the coconut shrimp. It was a little different. Instead of fried shrimp, it was cooked shrimp with a coconut sauce, broccoli and rice.

We finished dinner, had our fortune cookie and got the check.

"Shall we go back to the hotel," I asked.

"Yes, I'm a little tired," Mary responded.

"How about we stop by the bar for a night cap," I suggested.

"Ok, but not too long" she said.

"Ok great," I added.

We walked back to the hotel but didn't say much. Once at the hotel bar the bartender asked "what can I get for you?"

I looked at my wife and said, "Dear?" She asked for a Baileys Irish Cream. I asked for a glass of Chardonnay, my favorite. I could really use two but I'll be polite, I decided.

"Could I get another Chardonnay," I asked.

"You should really take it easy; you have a big day tomorrow. No one does well in court hung over," she added." she said.

"Ok, I will," I said.

After my second glass, I knew it was time to go. I left the bartender a nice tip and we walked to the elevator. I saw my wife's reflection in the elevator glass and thought damn, she looks hot, but I knew in my mind, there was nothing I could do about it. When we got to the room, I was so damn frustrated I felt like I could explode like an erupting volcano. Why the hell do I have to have ED. I hate this goddamn thing. I've tried all the pills and nothing works. It's a hell of a way to spend the rest of one's life.

When we got to the room, I put on the tv and my wife went to take a shower. I wish she asked if I would get in bed with her, but she didn't. Ok it's over, that's the end of my sex life. Even my wife isn't interested anymore. My wife came out in a sexy night gown. My daughter tells me that nightgowns are a thing of the past. I'm not sure about that, but it sure does something for me.

I said "How about if I take a shower and we get naked?"

She said, "Stop it. That's for young people."

Ok shutdown I got it. So, I took a long shower, get into bed and fall asleep.

The Trial – Day Three

I really felt like I got a good night's sleep. It must have been hat dream! When the alarm went off, I woke right up and was ready to go. Must have been because I went to bed horny the night before. I laid in the bed thinking about the events for the day. Not a whole lot left but a cross examination and testimony from the Pluriman CEO. After that wait is over it will finally be over. Hopefully with a positive outcome

My wife dressed in a beautiful black dress, silver high heels and a matching belt. I had on my black suit. We really did look like a power couple. "Don't over dress," my attorney advised. "The jury will get the wrong impression about you," he advised. Ok, I get it but these are our only clothes. I don't have a lot of suits anymore and my wife doesn't have a lot of dresses. After all we are older and don't go out to formal affairs anymore," I told him.

As we retrieved our car from the valet, we drove directly to the Courthouse. I need coffee I thought. We stopped at a street vendor and each got a cup of coffee. Boy it was almost as good as the Chinese dinner the night before.

We haven't had breakfast in days. When this is all over, I decided we would get a full breakfast at IHOP. We entered the courtroom and as usual, we were the first ones there. I guess it's the anxiety we are feeling that made me forget about breakfast. I was hoping that today would be the last day and we could get the hell outta' here. I want to go home. I've had enough, I told myself.

My lawyer comes in dressed in a dark green suit. Where does this guy get his taste, I wondered? I would never buy a suit like that. Ok, relax, roll with the flow, I said to myself.

Mitch approaches me and said, "I have a good feeling about today."

"Really why," I asked.

"Just a gut feel. I'm ready for the cross examination. Let's hope that Mr. Slick Shit is ready for me," he told me.

"All rise, the Honorable Douglas Bradford presiding," the bailiff announces.

"Mr. Whitman, could you could you please be seated in the witness box for cross examination by the Plaintiff?" the Judge asks.

"Yes, Your Honor," Mr. Whitman replied.

Then came Mr. fancy pants. He looked just as good today as he did yesterday.

"Mr. Whitman, let me remind you that you are still under oath" The judge stated.

"Yes, You Honor, I understand," he answered eloquently.

"Good Morning Mr. Whitman, my name is Mitchell Sildman and I am an attorney for the Plaintiff, Mr. Lindstrom."

"Good Morning Sir," he echoed.

"I would like to ask you a series of questions regarding the discontinuation of benefits for Mr. Lindstrom. Do you recall if Mr. Lindstrom was one of the Clients that was assigned to you," he asked.

"Yes, he was," he replied.

"Do you also recall that you discontinued Mr. Lindstrom's disability benefits," he asked.

"Yes, I do, but.," he replied before being interrupted.

"Thank You Mr. Whitman" Sildman says abruptly.

"Do you recall specifically what you told Mr. Lindstrom the reason was for the discontinuation of his benefits," Sildman asked.

"As I recall, Pluriman interpreted his request as a refusal to attend the doctor's appointment we requested," he answered.

"Did Mr. Lindstrom ever use the terminology "refuse" in any of his correspondence with Pluriman," he inquired.

"No, he did not" Whitman responds.

"Did Mr. Lindstrom request a postponement until a Covid-19 virus vaccine was available,' he asked.

"Yes, he did," he replied.

"Well, what was is it Mr. Whitman, a refusal or postponement. It can't be both, it's either one or the other" he explained as Sildman badgers Whitman.

"Objection Your Honor. We have already explained that a postponement is interpreted as a refusal" Rosen stated loudly.

"And I, Sir, have already explained to you that interpretations do not override the law. If you do not recall, I will have the court stenographer read it back to you," the Judge retorts.

"No need, Your Honor" Rosen said.

"Mr. Whitman, is a refusal the same as postponement in your mind," Sildman asked.

"Objection your Honor. The plaintiff is asking the witness to interpret legal documentation," Rosen claimed.

"Sustained," the Judge replies.

"Did you, Mr. Whitman, authorize a letter to be sent to Mr. Lindstrom to have his benefits discontinued," he interrogated.

"Yes, I did," he retorted.

"Did you also recommend that discontinuation to your law department," he asked.

"Yes, I did because Mr. Lindstrom did not adhere to the terms of the agreement," he explained.

"Really? I think he only asked for a postponement but was more than willing to go to the Doctor's appointment." "Isn't this true Mr. Whitman," he questioned.

"Your Honor I cannot answer that question because I did not make the determination," said Whitman.

"Sustained," the Judge replied.

"Mr. Whitman, isn't it true that Mr. Lindstrom submitted a letter to you requesting your Covid-19 policy," he asked.

"That is correct," he said.

"And what did you tell Mr. Lindstrom," he questioned.

"We were not at liberty to supply clients with our Covid-19 policies," he retorted.

"Well then, how were clients supposed to know what policies you had in place and how they should follow them," he questioned.

"I'm not sure, Sir," was his reply.

"Thank you, Mr. Whitman. By the way, did Mr. Lindstrom ask you to reinstate his benefits," he inquired.

"Yes, he did," he replied.

"Did you reinstate them," he asked.

"No, we did not," he replied.

"Can you please tell the curt why your company did not reinstate Mr. Lindstrom's benefits," he asked finally.

"Our lawyers felt strongly that Mr. Lindstrom was in violation of our contractual agreement," he replied.

"Mr. Whitman, to the best of your knowledge, does your contractual agreement have any provisions for Covid-19," he questioned.

"No, it does not," he replied.

"Objection, Your Honor, the plaintiff is asking the witness to comment on the legal comments of a corporate document," Rosen stated.

"Overruled, the plaintiff is only asking about awareness, not a definition" the Judge replied.

"May I ask why not," Sildman questioned Whitman.

"Yes Sir, the document was created before the Covid-19 pandemic. And Pluriman did not issue any updated documentation on Covid-19 for our client's but the company did issue guidance for employees and Customers," he stated.

"Why is that, Mr. Whitman? Why is it that Pluriman would issue statements about Covid-19 to everyone but their most important customer, the client?" he asked.

"I'm not sure Sir," he said cowardly.

"Mr. Whitman, I have in my hand a letter from Pluriman to Mr. Lindstrom dated August 26, 2020. Your Honor, this document is labeled Exhibit A6 which has already been introduced as evidence. In the client services response to Mr. Lindstrom, Pluriman clearly states, if I may read verbatim, "your request to delay your doctor's appointment is interpreted as a refusal and as such your case will be closed and your benefits discontinued." Mr. Whitman do you remember seeing this letter," he asked.

"Yes," he replied.

"Then once again, did you personally interpret Mr. Lindstrom's request as a refusal?"

"No sir, that came from our Law Department."

"Mr. Whitman, I will assume you had no objection to it because you reviewed it and let it go out. Is that correct," he asked.

"Objection, Your Honor. The plaintiff's attorney is asking him to comment on confidential company matters" Rosen stated.

"Sustained," replied the Judge.

"Ok, Mr. Whitman, let me remind you that you are under oath. During your employment with Pluriman have you ever had a client request a delay or postponement for a doctor's appointment," he asked.

"Objection, irrelevant to this case," Rosen called out.

The Judge said, "No Mr. Rosen, I will allow it. Sir, please answer the question."

"Yes Sir, there have been requests for delays or postponements," he stated.

"Were those clients always dropped as a result of their request," he asked.

"Objection, Your Honor, once again not relevant," he declared.

"Overruled. I find nothing inappropriate about this question. Please answer the question Mr. Whitman" the Judge said appearing to be annoyed.

"Yes, Sir, not in all cases," he replied.

"I'm sorry Mr. Whitman could you please respond in a complete sentence," Sildman requested.

"The clients were not dropped in all cases, however."

"Thank you, Mr. Whitman," Sildman stated.

"Objection, Your Honor. The plaintiff's attorney did not let the witness finish his sentence," he corrected.

"No. I'm satisfied with his response Mr. Rosen" stated the judge.

Sildman addresses Whitman, "So now I am thoroughly confused. You allow some clients to requests postponements and continue their benefits and others are dropped. There has to be another reason. Is it the amount of money you are paying them," he debated.

"Objection," Rosen stated loudly.

"Sustained," the Judge replied.

"Mr. Whitman, I would like to talk about ERISA Laws if I may. For the court, ERISA stands for Employee Retirement Income Security Act which was a series of Federal Laws enacted in 1974 to protect the disabled members of our population. That is the reason that we are here today. My client, Mr. Lindstrom, contends that the Pluriman Insurance company violated at least one of these laws. Mr. Whitman, are you familiar with these laws," he inquired.

"Objection, your Honor. My client is not an attorney" Rosen stated.

"Sustained," the Judge replied.

"Ok, Mr. Whitman, earlier you testified if I may quote you; "laws govern everything we do and are at the forefront of our company." Does that sound familiar Mr. Whitman," he asked.

"Yes Sir, it does," he stated.

"Then I must assume that you are aware that these laws exist," he asked.

"Objection, your Honor." Rosen called out.

"Overruled, please answer the question," he instructed.

"I am aware that these laws exist but it is up to our legal team to interpret and provide guidance for us. I do not interpret the law," he said.

"So, when your company drops some people and doesn't drop others, your legal teams "interpret" the law based on the claim," he asked quizzically.

"Objection, Your Honor," David Rosen shouted.

"Sustained. Sir there is no need to shout in my courtroom, Mr. Rosen," the judge responded loudly.

"I apologize Your Honor," Rosen said apologetically as he turned theatrically toward the jury.

Go, Sildman, go! You got this guy on the ropes, finish him off. This is like a prize fight. He's nailing that smug ass piece of shit. Game Over.

"Mr. Whitman, you told the court earlier that your criteria for managing your staff is based on them meeting their objectives, is that correct," he looked for clarification.

"Yes Sir," he said.

"And you also told the court that you supply each member of your staff with a number of individual cases to manage, is that correct," he confirmed.

"Yes Sir," he said.

"Mr. Whitman, did you or did you not have an established minimum or maximum case load for each client service representative," he asked.

"Yes Sir," he retorted.

"I'm sorry which is it, a minimum number or a maximum number," Sildman prodded.

"There are minimums and maximums assigned to the individual based on their grade level and number of years of experience," he explained.

"Thank you. And who established these numbers," he asked.

"I not sure who actually creates them in the company," he admitted.

"Mr. Whitman, do you ever exceed the number of cases assigned to a client services representative," he asked.

"Objection, Your Honor," Rosen declared as he arose to his feet this time.

"Overruled," the Judge responded.

"Occasionally we do," replied Whitman.

"Would this be the case with Mrs. Brown perhaps," he asked.

"Objection, Your Honor," Rosen shouted.

"Sustained," the judge replied in a sing-song voice.

"Am I right to conclude that one of your objectives for client service representatives is to close cases if the individual violated the contract," he asked.

"Objection, Your Honor," Rosen said.

"Sustained," the judge said wearily.

"Mr. Whitman, since it seems like you manage by the numbers, can you tell the court what percentage of disabled clients violate their contract," he asked.

"Objection," Rosen yelled.

"Mr. Rosen, I have warned you once about your boisterous outburst in my courtroom. If there is another incident, I will hold you in contempt," the judge declared.

This guy was clearly getting flustered. Sildman knew what he's doing. Man, this guy was good.

"Your Honor, may we approach the bench," Rosen requested.

"Yes, Mr. Rosen" the Judge responded.

Rosen spoke quietly to the judge, "The number that Mr. Sildman is looking for is highly confidential and provides our company with a distinct competitive advantage. I do not want to release it because it will become a matter of public record," he explained.

"I understand," the judge responded. "Mr. Sildman, I think I understand where you are going, but per Mr. Rosen's request, I cannot allow this question. Can you find another way to ask the question without using numbers," the judge requested.

"Yes, Your Honor. I will," replied Sildman.

The judge announces to the court, "The last question will be stricken from the record. Mr. Sildman will rephrase the question. I apologize for the interruption."

"Mr. Whitman do you keep track of the number of Clients that are dropped from disability," Sildman asked.

"Yes," Whitman replied

"Do you also keep track of the number of clients that each Client Service Representative removes from disability," Sildman questioned.

"Yes, I do," he replied.

"Mr. Whitman do you report these numbers to anyone else in the Pluriman organization and on what frequency," Sildman inquired.

"Yes, on a monthly basis."

"Mr. Whitman, can you tell the Court how many people you report these number to and their title? No names please.

"Objection" Rosen states.

"Overruled. We have discussed this issue already. Mr. Sildman is only asking about distribution. He has already testified that he does keep track of the numbers. Are we clear Mr. Rosen? Please answer the question Mr. Whitman" the judge requested.

"I'm really not sure of the exact titles because I use an email distribution list," he replied.

"Ok then, could you provide the court with a number range? Would you estimate it is more than 50 people," he asked.

"Yes," he replied.

"Are these individuals above your rank in the Corporation," he asked.

"Yes," he replied.

"Does the Senior Management and Chief Executive Officer receive this email," he asked.

"Objection," said Rosen.

"Overruled," the judge replied.

"So, would it be fair to say that most of your company knows what's going on in relation to the number of individuals that are denied disability benefits," he asked.

"Objection Your Honor, my witness cannot testify to whether an individual has read the email or not," Rosen said.

"Sustained, Mr. Sildman, would you please rephrase the question," the judge requested.

"Yes, Your Honor. Mr. Whitman, is it your job responsibility to both track and report these numbers to the corporation on a monthly basis," he asked.

"Yes Sir," he replied quickly.

"Thank You Mr. Whitman. No further questions, Your Honor," he finished.

"Mr. Whitman, you may step down," the judge said.

"Your Honor may I ask for a brief recess so I may consult with a witness," Rosen requested.

"Yes, Mr. Rosen, this is actually a good time. We will take a long recess and combine it with a lunch break. I would like everyone back in the Courtroom and seated by 1:00 p.m.," he insisted.

As Sildman returned to the table I couldn't wait to congratulate him on his performance. "Hey Sildman, you whipped the shit outta' him, way to go," I said as I contained myself from high fiving him!

"I don't want to get over confident but I think it went well," he assured me.

"I kept looking at the jury but they were expressionless" I said to him.

"Yes, they are really paying close attention. One more witness to go. This should be brief. It's the CEO and he's accustomed to giving speeches and spewing corporate bullshit. Don't expect much from him," he explained to me.

At 1:00 sharp, the judge returned to the bench. Man, this judge was as succinct as a military operation.

"The court is now in order," the bailiff announced.

"You are all reminded that you are still under oath. The Defense will call its next witness" the Judge declared.

"Thank You Your Honor. The Defense calls Mr. Charles Wilmer," he reported.

Mr. Perfect approached the stand and was sworn in like a new President during inauguration.

"Good afternoon, Mr. Wilmer," he said.

"Good afternoon" Wilmer replied.

"Mr. Wilmer, could you please state your title with Pluriman Insurance and the number of years with the Company," he requested.

"Yes Sir, once again my name is Charles Wilmer and I am the Chief Executive Officer for Pluriman Insurance. I have been with the company for 12 years," he stated.

"Mr. Wilmer, could you summarize your job responsibilities for the court," Rosen requested.

"Yes Sir, as most of you may or may not know, Pluriman Insurance is one of the largest Disability Insurance Companies in the world. We are a public company and therefore one of my primary responsibilities is to deliver positive return to our shareholders. But above all that, let me quote from our Company's mission statement, whereas Pluriman is responsible for providing affordable disability benefit programs to our business partners and to care for the health and well-being of our plan participants who we refer to as our clients. We have been in business for over 150 years and have a long history of supporting those individuals who have become disabled so they may maintain their standard of living as they recover from their disability and it is our hope that every one of our clients recover," he stated.

Ok I've heard enough. This guy should be a politician. I couldn't stand listening to this crap anymore, I thought to myself.

"Mr. Wilmer, in this court we have heard claims of your company, Pluriman, having quotas for eliminating disability payments for clients. Is this true," Rosen inquired.

"That is pure nonsense! We wouldn't be in business very long if we followed such practices. I will tell you that there are many disabled individuals entitled to the monthly payments we provide and unfortunately, there are those who take advantage of our generosity and supplement their income with our disability payments when, in fact, they have actually recovered from their illness or worse yet, they were less than truthful about their illness. I think this is where most people get confused about company quotas," he explained.

"Thank you, Mr. Wilmer, I think that clarifies our point."

"Mr. Wilmer, one of your manager's testified that he sends you monthly reports on the number of Clients that have been taken off the disability benefit ranks. Are you familiar with this," he inquired.

"Yes, very much so. As CEO I must keep my finger on the pulse of the corporation. The monthly report is one of the ways I can keep current. In my position, I need to develop future strategies for the company, identify trends that are taking place in the market and keep in touch using statistical data and information that I both share and discuss with my Senior Management Team. After all we are the guiding light for the Corporation," he said proudly puffing out his chest like a rooster.

"Thank You Mr. Wilmer." No further questions Your Honor," he finished.

"Mr. Sildman, your turn to cross examine the witness," the judge stated.

"Thank you, Your Honor," replied Sildman.

Ok, here we go, Round two of corporate bullshit. Let 'er rip!

"Good afternoon, Mr. Wilmer. Thank You for taking the time out of your busy schedule to attend this trial, as Sildman started his questioning.

"Of, course, this is important to our company and I wouldn't have it any other way," he blabbed.

Puke, puke, puke, that's all I could think of, but I had to keep a straight face and not showing much emotion.

"My name is Mitchell Sildman and I am the attorney for the plaintiff, Mr. Lindstrom, who is seated at the table over there," my lawyer started.

Wilmer smiled and nodded at me. I just wanted to wretch right then and there. What I wouldn't have done for a pair of earbuds, just then.

"If I may sir, just a few questions," Sildman asked.

"Certainly," he said with a smug smile.

"Mr. Wilmer, has Pluriman Insurance ever been sued before," he asked.

"Yes sir, we have been sued many times. It is a basic Constitutional right of all people," he said like a lying politician.

"More specifically Sr have you ever been sued by clients who felt as though you had eliminated their disability payments unfairly," he questioned appropriately.

"Sir, we do not eliminate payments. We have a very fine legal team which determines if a client is in violation of their contractual agreement," he explained.

"Do you recall, Mr. Wilmer, if any of these clients have won judgements against your company including Class Action Lawsuits," he questioned.

"Yes, I believe there were some but there are far more who did not prevail," he answered.

"Do you have any idea how many did prevail," he inquired.

"Objection, it is not my clients job function to track these types of statistics," Rosen declared.

"That's Ok Counselor, I would like to comment on that point," Wilmer stated.

Of course, you do, you piece of shit. Here I was trying to collect a pittance of disability and you and your fancy schmancy staff of overpaid lawyers are sucking down the bucks. How can you look at yourself in the mirror?

"Mr. Wilmer, I would advise you not to comment," Rosen declared.

"I understand, Mr. Rosen" Wilmer stated confidently.

"Mr. Wilmer, are you aware that there are a number of lawsuits currently pending in the courts where Pluriman

Insurance had violated the provision of the ERISA Act," Sildman questioned.

"Yes, there is always something pending however as a public company we are subject to this which is no different than any other company. After all Mr. Sildman, that's the American way," he finished.

"Yes Mr. Wilmer, it is as you say. By the way, I do have the numbers and every state in the United States of America has a lawsuit against Pluriman Insurance. In fact, there are more than 190 cases in the pipeline. I don't think numbers of this magnitude are the American way. No further questions your Honor."

"Mr. Wilmer you're dismissed. You may step down," the Judge ordered.

As Sildman walks back to the table, I was overjoyed.

"You are really something. You let him have it," I said.

"That was the plan all along."

"Do you think the jury bought his crap, I asked.

"No way. When I glanced over at them, I saw eyeballs rolling into their heads," he exclaimed.

"So, did I. What happens next," I asked Sildman quietly.

•

"Well, the Judge will charge the jury with their instructions. They will go off and deliberate and then return a verdict," he informed me.

"Do you think we'll hear today," I asked anxiously like a little kid in a candy store begging his parents for a little stash.

"If we're very lucky, yes, but most likely it will be tomorrow morning," he predicted.

The Judge begins to address the jury. "Before the jury begins their deliberations, I would like to give you instructions for you to follow in arriving at a verdict. In this case, the defendant, Pluriman Insurance Company has been accused by the plaintiff, Mr. William Lindstrom of violating the Employee Retirement Income Security Act of 1974. Mr. Lindstrom contends that Pluriman illegally discontinued his benefits when Mr. Lindstrom asked for a postponement in attending his doctor's appointment which was part of his contractual obligation. Both parties have submitted a number of exhibits which have been entered into evidence. Again, I urge you to deal with the facts of the case and do not consider hearsay or other comments made by the witnesses or their attorneys. You will be required to return a unanimous decision whereby all of you vote for the same verdict being guilty or not guilty. In this case as well, you will also be required to return a dollar amount of "punitive" damages. If, during the course of your deliberations, you need to have any portion of the court transcript re-read, please notify the guard outside of the deliberations room. Additionally, if you require a review of any of the Exhibits presented, please contact the guard as well. If you feel that you cannot arrive at a verdict by the end of day, please notify the Court and you may resume tomorrow. There is no time limit, however I would ask that you use your time efficiently," he instructed.

"Juror Number 1, please raise your hand. Sir, you are appointed as the Jury Foreman with the responsibility of guiding the deliberation discussions and resolving all issues. He and only he will be the individual that will return the verdict to the Court. This is a very serious matter and I will expect that you treat it as such. Are there any questions," he inquired.

"No, Your Honor," could be heard.

Ok, now the waiting game begins," my lawyer told me.

Sildman turned to me and spoke quietly. "You know, William, when you first approached me about doing a Jury Trial, I must admit, I was very hesitant but after listening to those corporate assholes, I knew we did the right thing. I felt a little like I did in my younger days when I was in love with the law and showed off my skills in the courtroom. I got some of that back this week and for that, I want to thank you very much, win or lose," he stated.

I could feel a knot in my throat and the tears started welling up.

"Thank you, Mitch, that means the world to me" I said proudly, like I had just won an Olympic medal.

I glanced back at my wife so I could wipe the tears, without anyone noticing.

An hour went by and no word. We didn't speak much. I just found myself looking around the empty courtroom wondering how many historic events took place in there. I kept playing back scenarios of the trial in my mind. One if we won and one if we lost. I am focusing more on the winning than the losing. After two hours I see the Judge leave the bench and go to chambers. In less than an hour he comes back into the courtroom. His black robe was flowing and he looked as though he had a scowl on his face.

"Ladies and gentlemen, the jury has not reached a verdict and we will adjourn for the evening. I am not going to sequester the Jury, but rather let them return to their homes and families. They are not allowed, under any circumstances, to discuss anything related to this trial. We will adjourn for the evening and reconvene at 9:00 am at which time, I expect everyone in their seats. Thank you, Ladies and Gentlemen. Good Evening," he announced like a defeated member of a baseball team.

Ok, back to the hotel it was. Same drill, different day. We retrieved the rental car and proceeded back to the hotel.

On the way my wife said "I think your lawyer did great today!"

"Yeah, didn't he," I replied. "He knocked those corporate assholes out and they didn't even see it coming. I'm feeling good about the outcome," I finished.

"Don't get too over confident now. You will be very disappointed if it goes the other way," she suggested.

"I know" I said.

We arrived at the hotel and zipped up to our room. I would have liked to stop at the bar but I followed Mary's lead.

"What do you want to do for dinner tonight," I asked.

"How about we get a drink first and then see if we can find a steakhouse," my wife asked.

"Yes, yes finally. I feel like we may be celebrating prematurely but I am dying for a steak, win or lose. "sounds good to me," I answered.

"Give me a few minutes to freshen up and the we'll go," she said.

I looked out the window over the city as the sun sets. Lights from the skyscrapers are beginning to turn on and there is something magical here. I look through the directory and find a Ruth's Chris Steakhouse within walking distance. That does it for me.

"Honey is Ruth's Chris Ok," I inquired.

"It's so expensive," she exclaimed.

"I know but I'm really in the mood," I implored.

"OK we'll spend our retirement money on a steak," she answered.

"Just promise me you won't get a salad," I demanded.

"Ok, no salad," she promised.

We stopped by the hotel bar. My wife had a Cosmopolitan and I had a Chardonnay. I am very predictable. We both downed them rather quickly and it was off to Ruth's Chris. It was only about a five-minute walk and the weather was good, like a typical spring day. When we arrived, the Maître D said that we had about a ½ hour wait. That's acceptable, I thought. Within 15 minutes, he called us for our table. Nice setting, nice atmosphere.

The waiter addresses my wife first and asked if she'd like a cocktail. Good for him, he gentlemanly asked the lady first unlike me!

"Pomegranate Cosmo" she requested.

"And for you, Sir," he finally asked me.

"He'll have glass of Chardonnay," my wife said firmly.

"Thank You, I didn't have to apologize this time" I said.

When the waiter came to take our order, I requested prime rib medium rare and my wife ordered the same except well done. Finally, I was beginning to relax.

"We don't talk much do we," I asked.

"No, you don't talk much," she replied.

Oh boy I just opened the gates for a fight I decided.

"You're right, I don't talk much," I said. Ok that will provide a little buffer. "I just wanted to say that I think you looked terrific today," I sucked it up with flattery.

"Thank you," she responded politely.

"I also wanted to say that I am proud that you are my wife," I admitted. I never tell her that enough.

"Thank you" she said.

"I also wanted to say that I Love You very much," I said. Shit, I am on a roll!

"Wow if this is the treatment I get when you get a steak, I'll cook one very night!" she said emphatically.

"No, seriously. I'm sorry but I'm trying," I said.

"I know you are and I appreciate it but it is not often enough," she told me.

"Ok, here I go, I'm sorry," I said.

"Why don't you get it, 'I'm sorry' doesn't fix things. I have feelings and I have needs but you are so much into your own world," she said. This was going where I didn't want to, like a foul ball!

I didn't know what to say. I am truly at a loss for words.

My wife responded, "Why are you such an asshole all the time? Why does it take a time away from home for you to be nice?" That was a good question if I do say so myself!

I don't know. I was really confused. Well, there goes that delicious piece of beef I was waiting for. Right in the crapper.

"I don't know what to say except I'm sorry," I said. I was beginning to lose the greatest feeling I was started to experience.

"That's your favorite saying and it's getting old."

"I wish you could have started all this before we got here. It would have been nice to address it at the hotel bar. I tried to do something nice and this is what I get. If you're waiting to ask me for a divorce that's Ok. I'm good with it," I blurted out.

"No, that's not it. I just want you to change. To enjoy life. To enjoy life with me. To do things we've never done before, to go places we've never been before. You know there's not a lot of time left and I want to do these things with you," she explained.

"Ok, I got it. You want me to change? I'll change."

"And what if I want you to change? Will you? No, don't answer, think about it for a while anyway I think our dinner's coming" I said out of frustration.

I was really not going to continue this discussion because there was no winning or losing. I'll shut up, take my lumps and did some serious soul searching. In the meantime, I am going to enjoy this prime rib no matter what. I really didn't give a shit if she doesn't like me anymore. Life is short and there's not a lot of time left. Wonder where I heard that before? I really wonder if other couples went through this? I thought things were fine and then whammy! Maybe we've been married too long. Maybe we need to separate. Maybe we need to divorce. Maybe it was all me, but what if it's her? No marriage counseling for me. Wait, maybe that's what she wants or maybe she just needs to get laid. Boy that is an excellent piece of meat, that steak, and I really don't care how hers tasted. She brought this shit on and I have nothing more to say. What a way to end an expensive evening.

We finished our dinner and passed on dessert. There were no words exchanged except "Ready to go?"

I couldn't wait to go to sleep and make this shit end. It was a very brisk walk back to the hotel and up to the room. I felt like I was taking a long walk off a short pier. I am really hoping that this was the last night we had to stay here. I was really missing my home. After washing up, I check the alarm and slipped into bed. I could feel the acid pumps in my stomach working away. Let me get an antacid and get to my dreams, I told myself.

The Verdict

As soon as the alarm went off, I got up and walked briskly to the window. It was a rainy day. My first instincts were that this was bad luck. Nothing good happens on a rainy day. But as usual, I hopped in the shower and got ready. Today was a little more casual so I am wearing a blue sports jacket, gray slacks a blue shirt and no tie. It doesn't matter at this point. What's done is done!

We checked out of the hotel, retrieved our car from Valet Parking and proceeded to the courthouse. There was no conversation with my wife. She was still be pissed off from last night, evidently.

Today I am going to get coffee. I asked my wife, "Would you like you get some coffee?"

"Yes," she said abruptly.

We stopped by a little coffee shop by the courthouse. It must be a popular place because the commuters were in and out. Man, I didn't miss those days. We got our coffee and walked to the courthouse. We went through the routine security screening and then up to the third floor. The guards knew us by now and greeted us with "Good Morning."

Since we were early, I asked my wife if she would like to sit down on one of the benches in the hallway. How noble of me huh?

"Yes," she said.

This was not looking good. She was definitely pissed. Time to break the ice.

"What time do you think we'll wrap up today?" I asked. This was beginning to feel like work.

"I don't know," she retorted quickly.

"Why are you so pissed off all of the time," I asked.

"Well maybe it has something to do with you. Do you think," she suggested.

Of course, it was always me. I was really starting to get very tired of this. Ok, we had our argument and it's over. Put it behind you and let's move on. But no. We have to play this silly ass game of not speaking for days and it gradually goes away. This was definitely not what I needed on top of this trial right now!

I spotted Mitch walking down the hall towards us. He stops by us and said "I have a good feeling about today."

"I hope so, Mitch," I said.

"Keep your chin up, it will all work out. I'm going inside to glance at the newspaper," he told us.

"Ok, see you in a few," I said.

After sitting for about 10 minutes, I said to my wife, "Let's go in now. I want to talk to Mitch."

"I think I'll sit out here" she said.

What she meant is that she will sit in the hallway so she doesn't have to look at me. That's fine. I get it.

I walked up to the plaintiff's table and asked "Mitch are you really optimistic? How are you really feeling?"

"Same as every other day. My joints hurt, I have a headache and my wife is pissed off at me. How about you," he said jokingly.

"Just about the same, but I don't have a headache," I answered.

"Well, sit back and relax. The end is near" he said.

At 9:00 a.m., sharp, the judge entered the courtroom.

"Ladies and Gentleman of the Court. Our jury is still deliberating so sit back and relax and we will notify you when they have reached a verdict," the judge announced.

For an hour I kept staring at my watch, but the time was going slowly. A few minutes before 10:00, a gentleman enters and walked over to the Judge.

"Ladies and Gentleman I am told that the jury has reached a verdict in the case. I will now ask them to reconvene in the courtroom," the judge stated like a champion.

A few minutes later the jury filed in and they were all expressionless. The jury foreman handed a note to the judge.

"Mr. Foreman, has the Jury reached a verdict," the Judge asks.

"Yes, we have, Your Honor," the Foreman stated.

Mr. Foreman, would you please read the verdict to the Court,' the Judge requests.

"Yes Sir," the foreman replied.

My heart was pounding and I'm sweating.

"Your Honor, we the jury find the defendant, Pluriman Insurance Company, guilty of violating the, ERSIA Act of 1974. We also find that Mr. Lindstrom's Long Term Disability benefits be re-instated with back pay to the month that the benefits were discontinued," the foreman declared!

Yes, Yes, Yes. Sildman, you did it! I couldn't contain myself. I glanced over at my wife an she was smiling. The Defense attorneys were in a huddle. Screw you, you bastards, I thought. Game over, I won!

"Your Honor, the jury also finds that Pluriman should pay the plaintiff $500,000 in punitive damages," the foreman continued.

"Oh my God! I couldn't believe it! We won!

"I guess this is it Mitch. We did it. I mean you did it. You whipped them like I've never seen before. Will I see you again," I asked.?

"I hope not," he said jokingly.

"Thanks again Mitch," I exclaimed.

It was time to depart. I went to see my wife and I hugged her like I never hugged her before.

"We did it. We won," I said.

"What are you going to do with the money?" she asked.

"Well, after I pay the taxes, I thought I would take you on that Alaskan cruise you always wanted to go on and we'll divvy up the rest and give it to the kids," I replied.

I knew both would make her happy.

As we left the courthouse, I knew the drive home would be quiet. My wife pulled out her cell phone and immediately called our daughter. That will keep here busy until we get home. Thank God no arguing for a few hours.

The whole way home I was reviewing the events of the week in my head. I As I drove, I kept replaying the testimony of those smug Corporate bastards. But what I thought most about was my stroke. Why did it happen? Was I destined to go to court? Am I really different than I was before? Only time would tell!

Unfortunately, there were no easy answers and like most, I will never know.

The Stroke

It was a Sunday, at the end of March 2018, another gray spring day in New Jersey. When I first woke up, I didn't feel good. It is hard to describe, but there wasn't one major thing that was bothering me. I had never experienced anything like this before, but it felt different this time. I knew something was seriously wrong. Over the past 10 years or so, I would have incidents of not feeling well and it would always be when my blood pressure was high.

We had planned a celebration that exact day for my planned retirement. All 3 kids and their spouses were going to come over about 1:00 in the afternoon. My wife told me in the morning that she wanted to go to the cemetery to visit her parent's gravesite. It was about a half hour drive and I really didn't mind going.

As we were driving, I started to notice problems with my vision but I thought, I'd shake it off. It was double vision and I would look up the list of potential diseases on the internet when I got home. I was really excited knowing that all of the kids were coming over in the afternoon to celebrate. Only one more week of going to this stupid job and I'm free. I didn't have any concrete retirement plans other than puttering around the house. I always wanted to write a book and I started one years ago. I wanted to learn the guitar and play the piano. I wanted to build plastic model cars and maybe get a train set. Yes, I wanted to do everything that I couldn't afford to do as a kid.

We got home around noon time and I told my wife that I needed to lay down because I didn't feel well. She kept asking what's wrong and I really didn't know. I never felt like this before. A few glasses of wine will fix me up I thought.

I woke up about 45 minutes later and I just still wasn't feeling right. The double vision was still affecting me but I couldn't wait to see the kids. Everyone arrived about 1:00 and Mary put out some snacks for everyone to munch on.

We recently bought a kitchen table that seats eight because the family was growing and our tradition is for everyone to be around the table. We had a little toast to my retirement and everyone was in a good mood.

I had just started drinking my wine when my daughter-in-law screamed out loud. They tell me that my left eye was sagging and my face turned purple. Although I was still experiencing double vision, I really didn't feel that bad.

My wife started screaming "we need to get him to the hospital. Call 911."

"No, we are not calling 911. I am going to take a shower and change my underwear" which I did. I knew they would strip me down at the hospital and I didn't want any skid marks in my underwear.

I don't remember much about the drive to the hospital or who drove me. I do remember, however, needing my son's assistance to walk into the Emergency Room. I had been to the Emergency Room with my kids many times before but never for myself. I remember my wife asking for my wallet while I was sitting in the waiting room. Then all of a sudden three nurses came out with a wheelchair to take me inside.

For most of my life I've been healthy. No broken bones, no stitches, no operation and no stays in a hospital. I don't like doctor's and I don't like needles. That's for sure. I think that I have a lot of bad memories from my childhood. I would always get deathly ill when I was a child. My mother would take me to our family doctor who would examine me and the ask me to lay down on the examining room table. He would go into the back room and come out with a needle. The Doc would say to my mother "I'm going to give him an injection of penicillin. He'll be better in a day or two." And then whammy. The needle went in my ass. Why did it hurt so much? Were the needles bigger back then? I always had a big butt so there was a lot of cushioning.

Once in the Emergency Room they got me on a gurney and I have no idea what they said. I do remember that they said I needed a CAT Scan and a few minutes later wheeled me into another room. As I look back, I can only remember certain things. And certain events.

I remembered them quickly wheeling me into the CAT scan Room. I also recall that the technicians were having an argument. Once inside, I remember the technician asking me my name, address and date of birth. This would occur continuously over the next two days.

The CAT scan machine was a big open ring and the procedure was relatively quick. I had no idea how much time had passed, but after short order, they wheeled me back into one of the ER rooms. As I was laying there, one of the nurses came in and said "Good News, it's not a stroke." Then I started to get upset because now I was wondering what the hell is happening to me!

Once again, I don't know how much time had passed but I remember my wife telling me I had to stay overnight. I don't like hospitals but I reluctantly agreed. I kept telling my wife to go home with the kids. The nurse told my wife they would call her when I got situated in a room.

It must have been about 7:00 p.m. when they wheeled me to an elevator to go upstairs.

When I got to the room, the nurses asked if I could get up and walk to the bed.

"No problem" I said as they helped me get to the bed.

The nurses were very kind and I remember one in particular asking me if anything was bothering me.

"Yes, the double vision is starting to drive me nuts," I said.

She said "We can fix that" and came back in the room with a bandage and tape. Placing the bandage over my left eye, she taped it in place.

"How's that," she asked. I looked like a fucking pirate, but what the hell, no skid marks at least!

"Great," I replied.

What a difference that made. She must have done it before.

After a little while in bed, I thought I should call Mary. Actually, I didn't feel that bad. I told her I was fine but just wanted to go to sleep. I gave her my room number and said goodnight.

I must have drifted off and a while later I was visited by a doctor with a bow tie. People that wear bowties bother me and I don't know why. He ripped off the bandage, grabbed my glasses and put scotch tape over the lens. I thought, what the hell are you doing, I don't wear my glasses except for reading but he didn't even ask. I remember some test he performed with a blue pen light but there was no discussion. He must have asked me questions but I don't remember what the hell I said.

God knows what they shot me up with or put in the IV. Several days later I read his report and it said that I drank 25 beers a week. I couldn't drink 25 beers in a year. I said to myself, this is not true. Yet this report becomes part of my permanent record.

This brings up another issue which has annoyed me for years. Why aren't all of my medical records in one place and why can't I see them? We have the computers and we have the technology. What's the problem? At 67 years old I still can't remember my blood type. I can't remember what I've been vaccinated for, but I do remember eating sugar cubes with pink medicine at school in the early 60's. (I think it was for polio). I remember the big scab on my arm after the Smallpox shot. I think I had the measles and chickenpox. Not too sure about the Mumps, but I do recall that they said your balls would swell and I would definitely remember swollen balls. As a child, every time I went to the doctor, he would give me a penicillin shot. God knows how much of that stuff I have floating around in my system. I don't even know if anyone studied the side effects of this in later years. Maybe ED is a side effect. Who knows? Just taking a wild ass guess because I don't understand why it won't work.

Anyway, I think we are moving in the right direction but it is very slow. Many doctors have their own websites or portals (God I hate that word "portals") for you to access your records. The only problem is that it only contains the information from that particular doctor. What the hell! I remember a professor in college giving an example about computers. He said, "If you are walking straight toward a wall, you will hit it at about 2 miles per hour. With a computer you will hit it at 100 miles an hour". Why I remember this, I don't know but it's still in there with all the other useless junk including old song lyrics. Bottomline is that I think we will get there someday but definitely not in my lifetime.

I was awoken several times during the night. The technician told me that the protocol for me is to take blood every three hours.

"You've been through this before? Right," the technician said before he stabbed me with the needle.

"No, I've never been in the hospital before and this is all new to me," I said.

He looked at me with a puzzled look and said "I'm sorry. Just a few more minutes and you can go back to sleep."

"Thank You" I said.

I woke up the next morning and I had a roommate. I couldn't see him but he must have been a real pain in the ass. He was constantly calling the nurses. At one point I heard him making a phone call asking someone if they could bring him cookies. I never did speak to him but I loved to watch the nurse parade.

About 7:00 a.m. the next day, the nurse came in and said "Good Morning". Mr. Lindstrom, you will be going downstairs this morning for and MRI at 10:00am."

I sort of knew what an MRI was, but this time it was for me. She explained that MRI stands for Magnetic Resonance Imaging. Basically, a giant magnet aligns all of your cells so they can take a clear picture to slice and dice. Unfortunately, you have to go into a tunnel with a plastic cage around your head.

"Is it painless?" I asked.

"Yes, completely painless" she said.

I understood that this was great technology and provided great results, but going into a tunnel is quite scary. There is no room to move and there is no space between your face and the top of the tunnel. People with claustrophobia must freak out. It would be Ok if this test was a minute but, I was in there for about 20 minutes with constant beating noises. I just kept thinking, what if the room catches on fire and everyone runs out and leaves me in here? But I guess that's a common concern of all patients.

When I got back to my room, there was a doctor already waiting. I thought, this can't be good. And it wasn't. At least it wasn't "doctor bowtie!"

The doctor said "the MRI shows that you've had not one, but two strokes. We can't determine when the first one took place but the second one is more recent. The technical name of the event is a Lacunar Infarction of the Thalamus which was brought on by high blood pressure. We will continue doing tests and will let you know when you can leave."

"Thank you, Doctor" I replied.

After she left, I thought I should call my wife and give her the news.

When I called Mary and told her, she didn't seem surprised. I guess everything was Ok then except for the double vision.

I asked her, "Do you think you can call the doctor and find out when I'm getting out?"

"Sure" she said.

Later that day, she called me and said "they need to do a few more test tomorrow and then you can go home."

"Thank you," I said.

I never really got upset while I was in the hospital. Why? I don't know. Any sensible person would be freaking out. I just had a stroke. Why am I not more concerned? Why am I not praying like hell to get better? Once again, it's one of those things I will never understand. Or, did I really die and this is just a dream?

I spent the next two days in the hospital being poked, stabbed and visited by a plethora of doctors.

The second day in the hospital consisted of a Thallium stress test. Another exciting event. Basically, they inject you with chemicals that simulate your heart being under stress. They take Xray's at certain points to monitor changes. The good news is that this test came out very good. So now we have eliminated the heart, it's only the brain that's screwed up.

Usually when I'm facing deep shit, I start praying. Yep, I am a phony. I only run to God when I want something or want Him to get me out of something. Funny thing, I don't remember praying at all. Not even when I was laying in the hospital bed at night with the lights out and that made me wonder if I was dead!

The stroke left me with a myriad of results which included double vision, severe fatigue and comprehension issues. Other than that, I am just fine. Luckily my limbs nor my speech was affected but people close to me tell me I'm not right, whatever that means. I can't drive anymore following an incident on a major highway when I stopped in the middle of traffic because I saw a tractor trailer going sideways. Fortunately, there was no tractor trailer and not a lot of traffic. I could have put a lot of lives in danger.

I would have never dreamed that I would have had a stroke. I remember that my paternal Grandfather had one at age 81, but he was old. I remember going to see him at Mt. Kemble rehab in Morristown, NJ. The staff was very nice and asked if I wanted to feed him lunch. What? I came for a visit not for lunch. The whole thing was a nightmare. They brought him to a table and handed me a cup of jello and a plastic spoon. When they wheeled him in, I was shocked. His words we mumbled and unrecognizable. I kept telling him that I didn't understand but he kept trying to talk. That was the last day I saw him before his funeral.

As is my nature, several days later I took to the Internet to better understand what the hell happened to me. Lacunar means deep within the brain. The definition of an Infarction is as follows: "an injury or death of tissue from inadequate blood supply. This may often lead to irreversible damage." Well, that's pretty scary. I read that there is a right and left. The thalamus regulates sleep and is also a relay to the cortex in the brain. So basically, there was an explosion of blood vessels deep within the brain. How lucky am I? No physical implications, but the mental ones were yet to come.

When I got home, all I wanted to do was sleep. Since it was springtime, I went out to do some raking. It couldn't have been more than 10 minutes and I was exhausted. Back to sleep again. I never really felt refreshed when I woke up. I could still respond to messages on my iphone and my speech was Ok. The damn double vision was really starting to bother me. When I would go onto the computer, I was having difficulty remembering what I wanted to do. I used to be a wiz at Excel with formulas and spreadsheets. Now I couldn't even type the numbers in. This was bad news. Here I was a few days away from retirement and this is how it's was going to start. I thought that when I retired, I could pursue my hobbies and do whatever I wanted. I always wanted to play guitar and piano. I wanted to learn a second language. I wanted to build model cars. I wanted to write a book. Now I just want to sleep!

I don't think my wife really understood what I was going through. I do think she realized when she took me for a Doctor's appointment and I kept crashing in to the medical equipment when walking down the hallway.

The hallucinations started a few days after my stroke. I remember seeing a man sitting on a wall with blue shorts and a white top. As I got closer, within seconds, I noticed that there was no one there at all. Other hallucinations included a red squirrel running across my front lawn and people walking toward my front door, but when I opened the door there was no one there. I was very reluctant to tell anyone about this even the doctor. However, during my next visit I found the courage to mention it to him. He wasn't surprised, but didn't say anything about it. This lasted on and off for a few months and then subsided. What a harrowing experience.

I think my memory remains intact but I am having difficulty with short term. My wife says that she has told me things and I swear to God I don't remember. But so, it goes.

I spent the next few months going to doctors, all of whom, would examine me and send me on my way. I kept looking for solutions for the double vision. I went back to the neurologist and he prescribed some medication which did not work. As I continued my research, I learned about "prism glasses." These are ordinary glasses but the lenses are constructed with angles that correct the double vision. I located a local doctor and made an appointment.

The day I arrived for the office visit; I was surprised when I saw that it looked like a regular optometrist office with frames for glasses on display. When it was my turn to meet with the doctor, they brought me into the examining room. Same chair with the eye equipment. I started to get really disheartened because I thought this guy was only going to give me a new set of glasses.

The doctor came in, sat down and asked me a bunch of questions about my stroke. Then he went into a drawer and pulled out a strip of different lenses. He held each on up to my eye and as he did, the double vision went away. Holy shit, I thought, this is a miracle. Then he said, "we can even make these to fit into your existing frames." I was ecstatic!

It was about two weeks and I went back to pick up my new glasses. I sat down in front of a mirror, out them on and to my dismay, there was no change in the double vision. I couldn't believe it. Even the technician was surprised.

The receptionist asked if I could stay and see the doctor to which I replied "yes". I have never been more disappointed and I took my seat until it was my turn. As the technician announced "the doctor will see you now." I muddled down the hallway. The doctor was already in the room looking at my glasses under some type of vision scope. He said "I don't think they gave us the right prescription. Let me re-examine you to confirm it." When he examined me with the glass strip, the double vision went away.

"Just as I thought, wrong prescription," the doctor said.

Yes, there is still hope.

"Do you think you can wait another two weeks," he asked like I had any choice!

"Absolutely, if this will fix it," I replied.

Two weeks later I got the call and I raced to the doctor's office. The technician came out and said, "Let's try again." I put them on and it was like a miracle. Unfortunately, years later, I still rely on them every day but I am happy to see.

Next it was off to Kessler Rehabilitation to begin my rehab program. Thank God my medical insurance covered it. I just hated that my wife had to drive me to rehab everyday but when I got there and saw some of the other people there, I was thankful. Very thankful that I had walked away from something that could have ruined the rest of my existence. I saw a 35-year-old guy that was completely incapacitated due to a stroke. I wish I knew more details. I consider myself lucky!

The staff at Kessler was fantastic! I can't say enough good things about them. They treated me well but at the same time they pushed me to regain some of the capabilities I thought I had lost. Everyday there was a new series of exercises and tests. There was one test in particular that I would do every day. Playing cards were stuck on the walls in two long hallways. I would walk up and down the hallway and read off the card that I saw. Never did get to 100 percent on that one but it made me think. I'm not seeing everything I should. Something is definitely wrong with me. To this day, it still affects me and I find that it has affected my ability to read and work on the computer.

About two months into rehab, the head counselor asked to speak with me. He said," Next week will be your last because the insurance benefits have run out."

"But I'm not there yet. I can't be finished" I said.

"I'm sorry but we must abide by the insurance regulations. I'm sorry," he said disappointingly.

"I know, it's not your fault. I just thought I was starting to do so much better," I cried.

"You are and I will give you exercises to do on your own to help you," he promised.

Disability

About six months after my stroke, I received a letter from the disability insurance company stating that my short-term disability was ending and that I may want to apply for long term disability. Since my condition really hadn't changed, I decided to apply for Long Term Disability. My employer had disability insurance with the Pluriman Insurance Company. No problem, there were no secrets and I have all of my medical records to support my claim. I kept all of my appointments and never missed or delayed one. I figured it was relatively straightforward. A traumatic brain injury supported by an MRI, neurologists, cardiologists, rehabilitation, neuro ophthalmologists and internist reports.

Several weeks later, I received a letter stating that Pluriman granted my disability payments for up to 5 years. All I had to do was go to the doctor once a quarter. Simple, however this was the beginning of the nightmare. The contract they asked me to sign was about 40 pages long. There were all types of terms and conditions but nothing of concern. There was one section; however, that stated that if I received a long-term disability settlement from Social Security, the entire amount was to be paid back to Pluriman. I thought, this is fair, I am repaying them for the benefits they paid me.

Attached to the letter was a report from the insurance company's internal doctor. It basically stated that after reviewing all of the various reports supplied by the hospital and doctors, the insurance company had concluded that I had a "rare condition". Their words not mine. So, they just confirmed what I had thought all along.

Over the next few months, I began receiving copies of emails to my doctors requesting medical records. I was wondering what was going on here, they have all of the information. At my next doctor's appointment, he told me that the disability insurance provider was asking if I could perform routine tasks and lift certain weights. Oh My God! I had stroke What are they talking about? I discussed it with my doctor and continued to report the same symptoms that I was experiencing. I am telling the truth here. Do you think I want to live like this? The doctor told me not to be concerned and he would respond accordingly.

Another month later, the insurance company asked me to meet with an independent representative "to better understand my condition". I started doing some research on the investigator and found that this representative was responsible for investigating insurance fraud. No fraud here I thought. I will be happy to meet with him. Bring it on baby!

On the day of the meeting, I welcomed him into my home and provided all of the information he needed. I asked my wife to attend also in case I forgot something. The meeting went well until he started examining my prescriptions and kept asking why one had less pills than the other. I told him that the doctors were trying different meds at different times. I asked him to look at the prescription dates and he could clearly see that they were all different but filled recently. What was this guy looking for?

When the representative left, I got a call from my neighbor across the street. He said "that dude has been taking all kinds of pictures of your house". What does that have to do with my claim? I went outside to confront him but he had gone. I quickly dashed off a letter to the insurance company expressing my distain for these tactics.

Now I knew what this was all about. He was interviewing me to see if he could find any lies or basis for fraud. Now I knew that I would be under surveillance.

Because of the double vision, my wife had to drive me around. Boy, how I hated that. Every time we would go out, I would be looking for surveillance people following us. This was like a bad spy movie I thought. I can't even go outside and rake the lawn for fear they would be filming me. What a way to live.

After a few months, it became evident that I could not no longer continue to maintain the home that we lived in for the past 20 years. We raised the kids here and continued through college until we became empty nesters. My wife was still working; however, the only income I had was from disability payments. We had planned and saved for retirement, but the property taxes were way out of control. I could not cut the grass anymore so I hired a lawn service. I couldn't do a lot of what I used to do, so I let things go. We had paid off the mortgage but the maintenance costs were more than I could afford. The time had come. We needed to sell the house. This was very sad because we raised all of the kids here. This was our dream house. This was our forever house. But it was not to be.

I don't know what my wife was thinking, but we spent several months looking at retirement places in New Jersey, Pennsylvania and Delaware. I was enamored with the model homes but in the end, I didn't like communities or the areas. I can't go through this. My wife located a 55+ community in southern New Jersey. I liked the models, but it seemed so far away from the area where we had grown up. I knew we could sell our house and pay off the new one off with enough left to let us live. We were basically homebodies and don't live to the extreme. We don't go out to dinner often or to even to shows. We don't have expensive cars. I try to do things myself instead of hiring someone, however even simple painting jobs were difficult. It was time to sell!

During the next several months I was copied on requests by the Pluriman Insurance Company for medical records. They had all of these records, what was going on? During my next doctor's visit, I found out why. The insurance company was asking questions to see if I could return to work and do my old job. Are they kidding? I had a stroke, a brain injury, a Lacunar Infarction of the Thalamus! Really? Now I'm starting to get it. They want me off the books and back to work so they don't have to pay any more. No concern for my condition, my quality of life or the fact that everything I worked for is slowly slipping away. Bastards!

Over the next few months, we made all of the decisions to build a house in southern New Jersey. It was sort of exciting making all of the decisions about roofing, siding, tile, lights, faucets etc. They said it would take about nine months and they were exactly right. No more lawn cutting, free gym membership, lifestyle trips and neighborhood parties.

It was in the Spring of 2019 that we decided to sell the house. We put it up in March thinking it would sell fast and at a price that our realtor recommended. For the next six months we lived out of a shoe box, keeping it 'showable' for potential buyers. We waited for people to see the house, but nobody came. We had four open houses and no one was interested. I was starting to panic. Friends told us we needed to buy little statues of St. Joseph and bury them head down on the property. Hell, I'll do whatever it takes at this point. I'll bury the holy family if I need to! We needed the money to pay for the new house.

Finally, during October, out of the blue, we received our first and only offer. It was a nice young couple and we were very happy to turn our home over to them. Everything worked out fine and they were just a great pleasure. Thank God that was over.

For the balance of 2019 the insurance company would send letters to all of my doctors to see if one of them would bite. Nobody took the bait, so in 2020, the insurance company turned up the heat. They were looking for any little loophole to get me off of disability. You see, I am a very honest person and if I didn't think I was deserving of disability, I would voluntarily remove myself from the ranks. But this is a brain injury. It isn't a cut that heals and goes away. Why couldn't I get through to them? Well, they already know that. My God, what about the poor disabled people who are in desperate need and get thrown off disability for some bullshit reason. How can these insurance people live with themselves? Don't they have a conscience? Don't they have morals? Don't they have a shred of human compassion for their fellow human being? I don't wish anyone ill and I hope to God that this never happens to them. I vowed right then and there to advocate for the disabled people.

I went for my regular doctor's appointment during the first quarter of 2020, but in March, I got the letter. The Pluriman Insurance Company said they were changing their definition of disability for all existing claimants. Instead of doing your old job, you would now be evaluated to see if you could do any job. Genius! Now they just closed another gap and can get more people off their roles. I do not mean any disrespect but visions of a store greeter were dancing in my head. I can't stay awake for three hours without needing an hour nap. How would I get to work? My God I'm 66 years old, not 40.

It was also during March that I found out that my Social Security disability appeal would be going to court within the next few months and I was prepared for the judge. I knew that all I needed to do is tell the truth. The funny thing is that the Pluriman Insurance Company put me in touch with another company that would assist with my Social Security disability appeal. Better yet, at no cost to me, except when you read the fine print. I would need to repay the insurance company with all proceeds from the settlement going back to them.

All was quiet in April and May but now the Pluriman Insurance Company's financial people were on my case. After the Social Security court hearing, I was granted a long-term disability settlement in the amount of $59,575. Now, the Insurance Company wanted their money back. They provided me with a letter that contained their estimates. I thought I would try and correlate the back payments with Social Security but that was next to impossible. After writing to Social Security and calling several times, I got nowhere. The financial people from the insurance company called a number of times wanting to know how much I received from Social Security and when would they be getting their money back?

In August of 2020, I received a letter from the Pluriman Insurance Company requesting that I see an ophthalmologist. What? I have already seen a number of ophthalmologists. The result was always the same. You had a brain injury and there was nothing we could do. The insurance company said that they wanted to better understand my condition. How nice of them! What they really want is for me to refuse to go, at which time they would terminate my claim. I sent the insurance company a letter asking for the name, address and phone number of the ophthalmologist. Initially they refused to answer stating it was a different area of their organization that makes the appointments. After much persistence, the provided the information I requested.

When I received their letter I thought, oh my God, the doctor was in the next state (Pennsylvania) in the heart of Philadelphia. As the crow flies or Google Maps it was 1 ½ hour trip on a good day. The insurance company did offer transportation. How nice of them. A little spent here gets a whole lot in return. Now I came to see that this was one of their own doctors. The company won't admit how they are compensated, but they are definitely on the payroll somehow. I searched the internet and found lots of information about "their" doctors. There was even a 60 minutes expose about the shady practices of the insurance company.

Here we are in the middle of a Covid-19 pandemic and they want me to go to another state to see a doctor which will most likely give me a glowing report card on how well I can see. The last ophthalmologist I saw was some old decrepit geezer in a wood paneled office with equipment from the 1950's. So, this is the scam. If you don't go, you get dropped. If you will see their doctor, you will most likely get a very positive report and back to work you go. If you can't get a job, you're dropped. If you do get a job, you're dropped. Checkmate!

I kept wondering what would the Pluriman Insurance Company do if I caught Covid-19 from the doctor's visit and died. The same answer kept coming back. Absolutely nothing. Therefore, I was assuming all of the risk. This guy is going to put his face right up against mine. What if he is asymptomatic? What if they don't clean the equipment properly after the last patient? After all, it has been my experience that these are not top tier doctors with state-of-the-art equipment. I requested Covid-19 policies from the insurance company and they would call me and tell me about doctors' protocols for Covid-19. Of course, nothing was ever in writing. The fact that the doctor has protocols, does not guarantee that they follow them. Protocols! Protocols! Protocols! Another word I hate. What if it's an Oops. Forgot to wash my hands or forgot to cleanse the equipment. Do I have any recourse? No. There's no criminal intent, just an Aw Shit!

By August of 2020, news reports stated that there were approximately 144 companies that had developed Covid-19 vaccine and there were a number of them that were in various stages of testing. Some reports even stated that the vaccine would be available to high-risk categories of people before the end of the year. Hey, that's me! I will step right in line and take my place. This will solve the problem. So, I took to the keyboard and scribed a letter to the insurance company requesting a postponement of my examination. Little did I know, this would seal the fate of my claim! Bite me!

The very next day I received a letter back from the insurance company stating that if I did not agree to the examination within four days, my claim would be closed and the benefits would be discontinued. They also had the nerve to tell me that there was no evidence of a vaccine. Are you serious? It's all over the news. The vaccine had already been developed, it's just in the testing phase and FDA regulations need to be followed. What set me off even more was the fact that the insurance company said, in writing, that my request was "interpreted" as a refusal and, as such, under the contractual obligations my claim was terminated. You can't be serious. I interpret this Insurance Company as a "piece of shit!" How can they get away with this! Aren't some regulators interested in doing something about this scam? What about the millions of deserving people that need these benefits and a thrown out the door like a piece of garbage?

I know that a lot of unsavory stuff goes on in corporations especially at the higher levels which are mostly impenetrable. What can I do at this point? There has to be something. So, I started to play by the rules. I'll play the "waiting game" if that's what they want but I just can't get over the fact that millions of people have accepted their flimsy responses and just turned away. I can't let this go. I need to do something.

I mulled thoughts around for the next few days and kept thinking that "the pen is mightier than the sword". So, I made a list of people that I would send letters to highlighting this injustice. Hopefully, I will get someone's attention and somewhere I might even find that they are breaking the law. Yes, their tactics were morally reprehensible, but I remember from my Law class in graduate school; because it's wrong, doesn't mean that someone is breaking the law. Ok I gotta keep focused on that as I move forward an put the emotional aspects on the side.

I started my journey by making a list of people that I would write to. The CEO of my former company, the insurance commissioner in my state, the Governor of my State, Senators and Representatives from my state. I would even file an Appeal with the insurance company.

I started by writing a letter to the CEO of my former employer letting him know about the methods and tactics that are used by their Insurance provider. Probably more of an awareness than anything else but it had to be done. Furthermore, he's a very smart guy, he probably knows what I'm talking about. He knew it was all about profit. Nothing new here. A few weeks later, I received a letter from the Human Resources Department saying that they would look into the matter. They even gave me the name and email addresses of the associate that would be handling the case. Holy Shit! It worked! I just couldn't believe it.

I immediately took to the keyboard and frantically scanned copies of correspondence from the insurance company. I wanted to make sure they heard my side before they contacted the Insurance company. Before the day was out, I sent all of the documentation to the Associate along with a brief letter of my issues. I didn't have to go any further. My old employer will do what's right. I knew they would. In an email response, the Associate told me that it would take two weeks to look into the matter. Wow, now that's impressive!

For the next two weeks I waited patiently for a response. How would it be worded I thought. Would they say "your benefits have been reinstated or we have reviewed you claim and decided that we would like you to attend the examination after you have received you Covid-19 vaccine." A few days later I received an email message from the associate. It was brief and said "we are sending you the results of our investigation by mail. You should receive this within the next few days." Crap! This can't be good news.

It wasn't. I couldn't read the entire letter after reading the first sentence that said "we find there was no wrongdoing". Are you kidding me! This whole thing stinks of wrongdoing. Let's take a deep breath and try to figure out what's going on. Any sensible person could see that this was not fair, not right and not moral. As such, the situation needed to be corrected. But wait, my old employer must be in cahoots with the Pluriman Insurance Company. Maybe there were kickbacks or discounts that need to be protected. Bottom line, I could not contain myself. I learned early on that when you get pissed off, you should take some time before you respond. I am breaking my own rule but what the hell. I once again took to the keyboard to admonish the associate for the outcome. I really didn't give a shit what happened because I have nothing to lose.

I thought the email I wrote to the associate was very good. I was calm, not threatening, but I think I got my point across. I told the Associate that I would be back in touch with the CEO. I also expressed my disappointment with the outcome and reiterated my points of contention with the entire issue. I figured the issue was closed like the end of a trading day on Wall Street and I should move on. I lost faith in my old company and told them flat out how they abandoned me in "my hour of need".

Next on my list was the New Jersey Insurance Commissioner. I knew that long letters rarely got read and would probably be passed off to some junior level person to look at. It wasn't easy to find out who occupied the position of Insurance Commissioner, but I finally found a name and address with a Trenton, NJ location. Here we go, I knew it was going into the bureaucracy barrel. Not much hope here. Just to make sure I was playing the game. I also file an "on-line complaint" with the Office of Insurance and Banking. Before I sent the letter to the Commissioner, I added that to signify that I was playing their game. While I am it, let me send a note to Governor Phil Murphy. I knew that he has more than his hands full with Covid-19 and budget issues.

Of course, the state did not disappoint. The Insurance Commissioner referred my case to New York, the Governor never responded and neither did the Senators or Representatives. I didn't expect anything and I didn't get anything. Ok where to next?

I am just a regular guy trying to right a wrong. I often think of how many other important causes there are in this world and I hope I can do something. Not for me, but for the millions of others who have already succumbed to this scam. And if you don't think it's a scam, take to the Internet and start poking around. You will find that it is a regular practice for these companies to close out claims. You will also find that there are awards and bonuses being paid for denying claims. You then won't be surprised at the number of lawsuits and past settlements. It's a numbers game. It's risk versus reward. The Insurance company has loads of tables, formulas, consultants and lots of lawyers to support their methods and tactics. If I am wrong, let me be the first to admit it! Now is the time to file an appeal with the insurance company, as is my right according to them.

Sure, I'm going to ask the company that just terminated my benefits to reinstate them. Am I crazy? After all this bullshit correspondence I know that a lawyer already drafted a standard response and they will sit on it for a few weeks to make it look like they're doing something.

I was shocked when I got a call from a nice lady from the appeals unit of the Insurance company. She said she was from Charlotte, North Carolina and wanted to know if there was anything I wanted to add to my appeal. You don't have to ask me twice. I explained that I never refused to go to their doctor but only requested a delay. I also told her that there was absolutely no language in any of their policy agreements that states that "a request for a postponement will be "interpreted as a refusal and as such, the claim will be terminated." Then she said. "we offered you a ride to the doctor." Now I know she just doesn't get it or is playing some type of slimy game. I politely asked why her company could not find an IME

(Independent Medical Examiner) within the ranks of 1200 plus ophthalmologists in the State of New Jersey. Next question please. I reminded her about the Covid-19 pandemic and the risks I would be taking. Next question please. Okay that's it. I've had enough. Thank you very much and goodbye. Really, they pay someone to do this?

Of course, I received the correspondence from the Pluriman Insurance Company thanking me for filing the appeal and speaking with them. Unfortunately, a week later I received another correspondence stating that they sent the information back to my claims handler and they see no change in their decision. I was furious. Where's the separation of duties, where's the Quality Control, where's the objectivity? But I was more upset with the nice lady. Where is your moral compass, where is your concern for your fellow man, where is you sense of right and wrong? Uuggghhhhh! Where is your sense of not being an asshole? But I never sent the letter.

I sent a letter to my Senator friend, a person I knew personally for at least 20 years. I sent an email to 60 Minutes suggesting that they needed to expose this crap. I guess my quest wasn't a newsworthy story. Never heard back from anyone. Not surprised. That's just the way things are. Just accept it. But I can't.

I stewed and stewed like a pot of boiling tomatoes and finally acknowledged that I hit a dead end and this was the way it's going to be. They won, they will continue to win and nobody will do a damn thig about it. Just a small guy trying to buck the system. My wife keeps telling me to fight the good fight but it's getting weary. I don't have anywhere to turn. I know, I will sue the bastards! So, I started my quest to find an attorney.

I have had dealings with attorneys over the years and none have really been positive until I won a case against my former employer. During the Discovery process however, I was shocked when I saw an email from one of the lawyers that I retained to another partner of the firm stating that he "should not to spend a lot of time on my case." What? I lost my job due to no fault of my own. The CEO was asking me to do illegal things that were against our "Code of Conduct". I brought the matter to our General Counsel, who I thought would help me. Boy, was that a mistake! I learned the hard way how tight the upper echelon sticks together. Nonetheless, I couldn't do what he was asking me to do. It wasn't legal, ethical or moral. Well, that was the end of my career, but we did settle the lawsuit.

I found lots of attorneys on-line and they were all over the country. Based on websites I visited, I contacted a firm that I thought would best represent me. They specialize in disability denial cases and their testimonies and interviews were impressive. Just what I was looking for. I filled out the questionnaire on-line and received the firm's brochures touting the millions that they have recovered for their clients. They said they would be contacting me within a few days to discuss my case. What they did, was to refer it to another firm because the dollar figure wasn't significant enough, I think. I understand this but they should have been forthcoming in their disclosures to state publicly that some cases will be referred. Passing the buck at its finest!

The referral company sent me an email with all of their firms' crap. Specifically, they would take 50% of back pay and a 1/3 of settlement. What? This is highway robbery, but I understand people need to get paid. Never heard back from them again. Guess they didn't want the business.

This whole thing was getting me depressed. I kept harboring negative thoughts. Who are you to take on this cause? You are nobody. Why don't you just sick back, enjoy the rest of your life? It will work itself out. Have you heard of Karma? Let the lawyers handle it. You won't get rich on the settlement if there is any. But what about this depression? Do I need to spend the rest of my life in this slump? I kept thinking of all the other people that have been unjustifiably denied. What about them? God Damnit! What about the disabled people?

In November 2020, I received correspondence from the Appeals Unit. They said that they could not make a decision on my appeal. They offered me to respond with any additional information. Once again, they copied the New Jersey Department of Banking and Insurance to no avail.

My wife and I continually argued about how I should respond to the insurance company. She wants me to go back in history and cite quotes from doctors' reports. Worthless, I thought. She also wanted me to call them. Calling won't get me anywhere, but I needed to respond. This time, I will make it really simple. In my letter I wanted to make clear the issue at hand. I stated that the Insurance Company dropped me because I made a request for a delay until I could get a Covid-19 vaccine. Short and simple. Oh, and I also asked them to cite in their documents where a "request" may result in closure of the claim. In their letter, they also said that they may need an additional 45 days. Ok you're not wearing me down anymore. I have nothing but time.

I was just waiting for the denial of the appeal so I could contact the Attorney and get the lawsuit underway. Most of the lawyers said that these types of claims usually took 12-18 months to resolve. Of course. Should I expect anything different?

I contacted a lawyer from a small firm and asked if they could handle my case. I spoke to a paralegal who advised me to file the appeal and then call the firm back when they denied the appeal.

No less than two days later, I received the final denial for my Appeal. I sent a letter to the insurance company asking if they could supply me with their document that contains the references to dropping claimants based on the fact that the claimant made a "request." Of course, they didn't supply it, but did supply seven pages of gibberish. There is no way they could have done this in one business day. It was already prepared. Do they really think I'm that stupid? I guess so.

Now we'll continue on the legal route again. After I received the final denial of my appeal. I called the firm back that I had spoken to before. When I spoke to the paralegal, she asked me to fax a copy of the denial letter so she could present it to an attorney for review. Since this was a smaller firm and I thought they might be hungry for the business. Late Friday afternoon I received and email to set up a conference call with their attorney for 9:00 a.m. Monday morning. All weekend I prepared with a factual brief summary of my case. I knew their time was valuable and I kept it brief and to the point.

At 9:00 a.m. on Monday morning, the attorney called me. He asked if he could call me back in 10 minutes. "Sure" I said, I had nothing else to do. Ten minutes later he called back and asked me for a summary, just as I had planned. I went through the whole spiel and finally asked, "so do I have a case?"

There was a brief silence and then he said:" I wish you had gotten me involved before you filed the appeal. I could have written a letter citing conditions of your case."

I said "Just so you know, I did call your office before I filed the appeal and the person told me to go ahead and file the appeal and then call us if you get a denial."

"Who did you speak to," he asked.

"A paralegal, how many do you have," I inquired.

No answer, just silence. He said "let me give you the name of someone in your state that may be able to help you."

I really didn't get it. These lawyers advertise that they can help anyone across the country. Why does the lawyer need to be in my area? I know. It was the bums rush to get me off the phone. It all makes sense now.

I wrote down the name and number he gave me, but I was pissed. Your office gave me bad info, I thought. Shouldn't you try and make it right? But they didn't. I can't help but think that there is not enough money involved. Why won't they tell me the truth? I am getting confirmation on why people have such distain for lawyers.

The same day I went on-line to look up the information of the lawyer he suggested. Same old crapola. Disability lawyer blah, blah, blah with years of experience blah, blah, blah, wants to help people blah, blah, blah. Filled out the on-line form and within an hour I got a call. Guess who? The paralegal. She asked all kinds of questions and asked me to send the Appeal denial. Now I waited to see if the attorney thinks it was worth it or not.

I mulled for a few hours and thought to myself, I give up. That's it, it's over, I've had enough. Sitting at the computer I decided to do a search on the lawyer he recommended. A one-person practice about 125 miles north of where I'm located. Probably needs the money. Profile says she's in her 60's, so she's probably getting ready to pack it in and needs to coast a little bit. Let me give it a final shot.

Finally, on the second day, after my initial contact, the phone rang about 2 p.m. Damn, it was the lawyer. She started by asking me about the referring lawyer like she didn't know who he was. From his description it sounded like they were buds. Then she asks why he didn't take my case and I explained the conversation. She was looking for the vaudeville hoop to end this quickly and then she blurted out, "I think I am going to have to decline as well. I will send you a letter. Thank you very much for contacting my office."

Wow that was fast. Not even a chance for me to say screw you.

So now it's finally over with the lawyers. I stewed for a few days and Thanksgiving was coming up. Why can't I just let this go? It's not about the money, it's the principle of the thing. And then I heard it loud and clear. Because it's not right doesn't make it illegal. The unspoken answer was; there's not enough money in this for me to waste my time on you! What a punch in the gut but I always come back fighting!

On Thanksgiving Day, I start my internet search again changing up the key words and phrases I use to search. Right off the top I hit on two law firms that interested me. I filled out the on-line form and that very same day, I received an email from the lawyer saying he will call me tomorrow. Wow, I am impressed. But he never called. A few days later, I get an email from the other lawyer. He asked if I could send him a copy of the appeal denial letters, which I did. A few days later he calls with no advance warning. I was really preparing myself to listen and then get the vaudeville hoop.

He didn't want me to summarize but it was evidently clear that he has read and absorbed all of the detail in the denial letters. One of the first things he said was "I don't know if I'd want to be in a car with a guy, I don't know, traveling to a doctor's appointment in the midst of a pandemic."

Holy Shit! This was the same thing my wife has been saying all along. I didn't even think it was relevant.

Since I'm at the end of my rope I said to the lawyer, "Listen, I'm worried that there's not enough money here for you. If that's the case, could you tell me now so we can both move on?"

He startled me by saying, "Let me worry about that. Here's what I'd like to do. I will contact Pluriman and ask for all of your records. Then I will take one day, sit on the couch and read through all of them. At that point, we can see if you have a case. How does that sound," he asked.

"Sounds good to me, but how much will this cost me," I asked.

"Absolutely nothing. This is part of my job," he responded.

One other question. Have you ever sued Pluriman before?" I asked politely.

"Yes, I have. As a matter of fact, I have two other cases against them now," he informed me like a proud parent.

"Ok, let's do it then," I said.

We started the same day with my signature on a form to release records. Man, this guy isn't wasting anytime. He sent me an email with his terms and conditions. He also let me know that it may take a few weeks to get through all of the records. Ok, let's play the waiting game. I got the message, I'm at the bottom of the food chain so to speak. Christmas is coming and I'll contact him again sometime in the new year, I decided.

Two days after Christmas, I received a phone message from the lawyer saying that he has reviewed everything and we're ready to move forward. I couldn't wait to talk to him. The next day we connected via phone.

He said, "I think we should move forward with the lawsuit but I wanted to go through four possible scenarios to set expectation."

"Ok," I said.

"First, there is such a backlog in the courts that the Judge may just throw it out. Second, the Judge could remand it back to Pluriman to settle. Third, Pluriman could offer us a settlement or fourth, we go into the system for a jury trial which may take years. How do you feel about the options," he asked.

"Let's move forward. I understand the options and I have nothing to lose at this point" I said.

"Great. I will prepare the paperwork for the lawsuit. The filing fee will be about four hundred dollars," he stated.

Cha-ching I thought. Here we go. I may be in for the ride of my life!

After I hung up, I started having second thoughts. Who is going to stand up for what's right? Me? I have never done that in my life. Why start now? This can be nothing but trouble. There is no upside to this fight. Maybe it could cause another stroke. A more severe one this time. I have no support and the family thinks I'm crazy. Maybe I'm doing the wrong thing. But what about all of the disabled people? Someone has to give a shit!

Over the next few days, I contemplated my decision. What am I going to do while this whole thing goes into the system? I know, I'll write a book about it. Yeah, I always wanted to do that! I'll write a book about these insurance scams and expose all of them. I'll tell people how I won my case and let them know that they can do it too. But, wait. I am mentally compromised and how will I ever work on the computer again?

The Book

I have never written a book before, so I cruised the Internet and started researching book writing and publishing. As I started my research about publishing, I was stunned by two facts. First, I found is that a book should be comprised of about 90,000 words. I don't think I've ever spoken that many words in my lifetime! Second, expect that you will probably only sell about 50 copies (to friends and family) and it won't be worth the investment. What concerns me more is my audience. Who really cares about this shit? No one, I thought. Maybe I could donate the proceeds to the disabled who have been screwed by these companies. But that won't fix the problem.

I just couldn't let go of this idea and I was becoming obsessed with it. Now it's time to face the computer. No family coming to see us this year courtesy of Covid-19. I need to occupy my time somehow. What better than therapeutic writing to get me through this pandemic.

Because of my condition, I knew that it would be difficult to put together some semblance of cohesive thought. I didn't even remember how to uses the keyboard anymore. I'll try it and if it doesn't work out, I would just give it up. But, that's not in my nature.

It's both helpful and customary to start a project like this with an outline, however I just started pounding the keys. I wanted to get my thoughts on paper and my mind was going a million miles an hour. I would do a little bit each day and before my naps and going to sleep at night, I would think about the structure and how the whole thing would play out.

I must be weird, but once I write something, it's difficult for me to go back and read what I wrote. I will wait until I am forced to proofread before publishing. As for the words, I am nowhere near the 90,000 and I don't want my audience to read a bunch of fluffy junk just to meet a word count goal. It is what it is. Who knows, maybe I'll only get about 12 pages and it will turn out to be a children's book, but I really didn't want to be a children's book author!

I finally developed an outline which gave me structure. Almost every day for six months, I wrote something for the book and what an experience it has been. I would rather write than speak. And when I write, I like to do so the same way that I speak. In a conversational style. So now you understand. There had been days that I wrote 10 pages and days where I can't even look at the keyboard. Before I go to sleep at night, I think about things I should be writing about. In most cases, they are not worthwhile. All of the time I think about my readers. Will they understand my sense of humor? Will they understand the way my mind works because I sure as hell don't. Most importantly, will it help the cause? Will it help to expose the shit that goes on in these corporations and the thousands of people that suffer directly as a result.

I worry allot about what a publisher thinks. Will they like my style? Do I curse too much? Is my grammar good? Is my punctuation correct? Am I boring? (yes, according to my wife). Are my paragraphs, right? And the list goes on and on. Anyway, it's done. Now all I have to do is read it and make corrections. I estimated that it will take me about a month. But it took much longer. I had to check my spelling, my punctuation and my facts. I found a book in the closet which I used as a guide. It had a price sticker on it for $24.95 so it must be a good book.

After formatting, cutting and pasting, I prepared the manuscript to send to the publisher. I got the names of Publishers who specialize in first time authors from the Internet. I really don't understand how this whole thing works. I guess I'll find out as I go along.

After polishing the manuscript, it was time to send it to the publishers. I have selected 12 of them fearing that I won't get a response from half of them. I also set up a second email account so I can communicate with publishers and the like. After I sent off the manuscript, I waited and I waited like an expectant father in the delivery room! I knew it was a piece of shit.

Days turned into weeks and weeks turned to months. And then one day I got a call. He sounded like some "low life" with a bit of a southern drawl. He asked to speak to me and I acknowledged.

"I read your manuscript. It's Ok I guess, but, Son, you just put a heap of shit on yourself," he said.

Who is this loser I thought? How dare he tell me that my months of slaving over a keyboard is just Ok. Furthermore, I'm not his son. Right now, I'm a lot on the defensive side like I was in the courtroom.

"First of all, I'm not your son and second of all, what the hell are you talking about," I asked.

"You never wrote a book before have you," he inquired.

"No," I said sheepishly.

"You don't understand how this whole thing works do you," he inquired.

"No, I'm sorry, I don't. Can you help me out and explain what's going on," I asked.

"Sure thing Cowboy," he says with that annoying southern accent. "What you just did was open a can of shit on the Insurance Industry. You basically exposed their scummy tactics and told the masses how to beat them at their own game. Are you hangin' with me so far? You are going to cost them tens of millions of dollars and they don't take kindly to that. As a matter of fact, I imagine that they will open a can of whoop ass on you," he finished.

What the hell was going here? I really didn't understand. This guy is a nut job. Maybe he was not a publisher but an insurance guy in reality?

"Hey, I don't really understand what you're talking about and I think you're full of shit. So why don't you just tell me why you called," I said emphatically.

"Believe me Son, I'm only tryin' to help you out of a shit storm that's a brewin'. Once these insurance dudes get word that you're gonna publish this book, they be a gunnin' for you," he informed me.

"Ok, I'm not afraid of any lawsuits because I didn't use any names. And by the way, it's classified as fiction. So, what are they going to do? Send me nasty letters from their overpaid lawyers," I said.

"Oh boy, I'm gunna' need to educate you. See here's how it works. You sent you book to a number of publishers. They in turn give a heads-up to their contacts at the insurance company. Then you be on the radar. The publisher gets some cash and you be on the stinky side of the stick," he explained.

"What the hell happens to me," I asked.

"Well, they will start messin' with you right away. They will know everything about you and your family," he finished.

"Wait a second, this has nothing to do with my family" I replied.

"That's what you think!" Ha, ha, ha. you got some choices to make Son. I ain't makin' a dime off this call, only doin' you a favor," he said with a chuckle.

"Ok, Ok, what should I do," I asked in earnest.

"As I sees it, you can pull the book and go back to livin' your life, or you can proceed forward and it may cost you your life. The choice is yours my friend," he told me.

"I need some time to think about this. Can I take a few days to think about this and call you back," I asked the southerner.

"Well, most certainly but don't wait too long because the shit storms a comin' soon," he said.

"Thank you, I really appreciate your call," I told him as hung up.

Now what the hell should I do?

I spent the next two days going through all types of scenarios. I really needed to discuss this with my wife but she will probably think I'm crazy. But it needs to be done. On the second night after dinner, I said to my wife, "we need to talk about this book thing," I told her.

"Ok, how much is it going to cost us now," she said.

"It may cost me my life," I said.

She laughed out loud. "It's only a stupid book and probably nobody will buy it. I think the only reason you're writing it is to feed your ego that hasn't been fed since you left your job," she explained.

I went through the details of my call and she said "Honey. Don't you see, you've been scammed! This guy doesn't want you to publish for some reason. Why don't you concentrate on figuring that one out," she suggested. Maybe she had a good point there.

I bet she's right. The more I thought it over, the more bizarre it sounds. Screw him, I'm going forward. I don't know what he's up to but he is off my list and I am not calling him back. I don't need any more mental torture. I really didn't think about it anymore and just waited for the other publishers to call. But, two days later, the phone rang.

I looked at my caller ID and I know it's him so I'll bite. "Hello," I said.

"Hey Son, I didn't hear from you and was a wonderin' what you decided," he asked.

"Listen, I don't know what you angle is, but I don't believe a word of your bullshit story. Furthermore, don't call here anymore" I said authoritatively.

"Okey dokey. You've been warned. Good Luck! Nice knowin' ya," he said before I heard the 'click' of him hanging up his phone.

Well, that was over with. Thank God.

About a week went by and out of the blue my wife said; "I received a very strange call and I want you to listen to it. I know you haven't left the house so I know it's phony."

So, I listened to the message. "I hoped your husband liked the sex and tell him it will be better next time, I promise. Call me. See you soon!"

Oh My God. I looked at my wife in disbelief. "You know this isn't true? Right," I vehemently stated.

She said "I know it's not." But I could tell there was something rattling in the back of her mind, like a snake in the grass!

Maybe it was a joke. Yeah, that's it. It's one of my stupid friends, but this is way beyond a prank. This is bad. Maybe it's someone who is in love with my wife and is trying to break up our marriage. Far-fetched, but stranger things have happened. Now my brain is on overload.

Every night before I went to sleep, I lay in bed thinking about things. Because of the stroke, I usually go to bed about 8 p.m. and my wife stayed up to watch her stupid shows. Usually, I reflected on my childhood and replay the good times but tonight was different. Oh my God, it's happening. It's just like he said. It started slowly and then they will ramp it up. It's way too late now. Everything is in motion. I can't stop the publishing now and if I do, it will be a huge financial loss which I really can't afford. Worse yet, how do I tell my wife. It certainly won't be a pleasant discussion and I'm not looking forward to it. What am I going to do? I am going to let it go. I've built a mountain out of a mole hill. Nothing I can do about it. Relax, I thought. Don't think about it but it keeps popping into my head. I am torturing myself. Stuff like this must happen to other people. I can't get to sleep. As is my nature, I need a plan and I need it now! My mind was racing a million miles an hour.

I got out of bed and entered the living room to talk to my wife. "What are we going to do about this? It's really bothering me," I admitted.

My wife laughed. "Wait until she calls again and I'll put you on."

"Seriously?" She started laughing again. "I haven't given it a second thought. It's probably a crank call from one of your stupid friends or a misdialed number. Go back to bed and go to sleep. It will be better tomorrow," she tried to assure me, but it didn't work. This wouldn't sit right with me until it was resolved.

I tossed and turned all night like a bread maker kneading its dough. The acid pumps in my stomach were on full blast. I must have been up three times taking stomach meds. Please make it stop. Maybe if I prayed, it will go away. I'm starting to think I was a schizo. But finally, it's off to lala land.

When I woke up the next morning, guess what? It's the first thing that pops into my head. I was tired and cranky with not a lot of tolerance to deal with this thing again. Per my usual routine, I got up, cleaned up, grabbed a cup of coffee and saw what going on in the world. I check my Facebook, my email and my checking account. Gotta watch those cyber criminals.

There wasn't much in my secondary email book account except the correspondence with the publishers. I usually don't read the junk emails but there is a new one there that grabbed my attention. It has a title of; "Wife's phone message." What the hell? Do I open it? Is it a virus or a trojan or ransomware? I had enough security on my computer but I needed to read it. I know, as soon as I opened it, bam, it was all over.

I clicked on the email and began reading. "Did you hear the voice mail we left for your wife? This is only the start and there's more fun to come! But you can make it end. You know what you have to do. Do it or buckle up, Cowboy," he said

Holy Shit! What do I do now? I know enough about computers to be dangerous but I don't know how to track the source of an email. Maybe, I should call the cops. They will probably laugh when I tell them about my wife's voice mail. I know, I call my buddies in IT and see if they can help me out. I really only had one or two I could trust and they both had full time jobs in corporations but it was worth a shot.

Wait. Something was bothering me about this email. It's really not a threat but the person calls me a Cowboy. Who else does that? Yes, that son-of-a-bitch publisher that called me. He just gave himself away. Plus, he used my secondary email address that only a few people have. I've got him now or did he want me to catch him?

I was spending a lot of time thinking of how I would handle this email situation. I hadn't told my wife about it yet and I was definitely not calling the cops. But I will call my buddy Bill and he if he can track down the source. Then I can wrap this whole thing up. I envision going to this guy's office but what am I going to say? I was certainly not going to threaten him. Maybe I should take one of my pistols and put it in my waistband so he can see it while we had a discussion. Maybe, I should just call him and say "gotcha" but there were no consequences. I don't need to decide this now. Let's see what my buddy Bill comes up with, I decided.

"Hey Bill, what's up? I called to ask for a favor. Can you track the source of an email I received," I asked.

"Sure, why," he asked.

"I got this email. It's very strange and it's bothering me," I said.

"Sure. Shoot it to my personal email, not my work email and I'll find out for you. Is it a girlfriend," he asked. What an ass, I thought. He knew me well enough to know I'd never cheat on Mary.

"No stop it. You know that book that I was always going to write? Yeah, well, I wrote it and there is strange shit going on," I informed him.

"Ten-four good buddy. Give me a few hours and I'll call you with the diagnosis," Bill replied.

"Thanks, I really appreciate it. Talk to you later. Thanks again," I said.

Now let me get the phone number from that son- of- a -bitch publisher. So, I went into received Calls on my phone and there it is but something didn't look right. The area code doesn't look right. Oh well. I was in the cat seat now. My day has just gotten so much better. I still got it!

A few hours later my cell phone rand.

"Hey buddy! Bad news. It's not traceable," my friend Bill said.

"What do you mean," I asked.

"Whoever sent it is using cloaking software just like those cagey North Koreans. No way to trace it. I'm sorry but I ran it through the very best software we have. Sorry. Hopefully she'll call you again. If not give her my number," he said jokingly.

"Ok would you please stop it! Thanks for your help. We'll hook up soon. Really, I do appreciate your help. I owe you one. Ok Bye," I said.

Shit, Shit, Shit. Ok, now I am going to call this bastard and confront him and I am not even going to rehearse. I went into the den and dial the number and wouldn't you know it, a message comes on and says the number you have dialed has been disconnected. Please try your number again. Isn't that my luck! Now what do I do? I went to the Internet and started looking at the emails this son- of- a- bitch sent me. Then I started searching for his office phone number. Bingo, I got it. Time for another call.

I frantically dialed and on the second ring a woman answered, "Morrison Publishing, Elaine speaking, how may I help you?"

"Hi, my name is Bill Lindstrom and I submitted my first manuscript to Mr. Morrison. I'd like to speak with him."

"Certainly, one minute please. Could you hold for two minutes? Mr. Morrison is wrapping up another call and he always likes to speak to aspiring authors" she said politely.

"Thank You" I said.

About 2 minutes later a voice comes on; "Art Morrison speaking may I ask who's calling?"

"Yes, Mr. Morrison this is Bill Lindstrom and I submitted a manuscript to you about 2 months ago."

"Oh yes Mr. Lindstrom, I apologize but I am not all the way through it yet and it is my policy not to call the Author until I have finished it. What's on your mind?"

"You don't have a Southern accent" I said confusedly.

"Never did. Never will" he chuckles. Sir, I promise I will finish your book in the next week or so and then get back to you," he finished.

"But you called me a week ago," I told him.

"I beg your pardon Sir, but I believe that we have not spoken before today," he informed me.

"I'm very sorry, I was just checking in. I know that you are very busy but do you have any feeling about my book so far," I asked.

"We'll speak soon. This is your first time publishing a book, right?" he asked.

"Yes, it is sir," I said.

"We'll talk soon but if any of those other publishers call and try to sell you a bill of goods, call me first, Ok," he implored.

"Yes, Sir, I will. Thank you very much for your time."

What the hell just happened? I never spoke to this guy before. He didn't have a Southern accent and not once did he call me "Son". Something was very odd. Someone was playing with me or there is a real conspiracy going on. I need to do more research on this guy and his firm to see if there has ever been any funny business going on. So, it was off to the Internet again.

As I searched on Art Morrison, I couldn't find anything. I kept searching and searching with no results. Then, I tried Art Morrison Publishing and there are pages of references. I perused through each one of them and there is nothing bad. Even the Yelps and the Google reviews were good. Maybe it's me. I'm screwed up. I must have been confused. I need to backtrack and start again. Mr. Morrison must have thought I was nuts. Yeah, that's it. Dementia or Alzheimer's is setting in. My mother had Alzheimer's so it's genetic. Let me go to the Internet and see what tests are available. Wait. I'm sick of the Internet for today. I need a glass of wine and relax.

You know what? I decided that I'm going to take a day off from the Internet and "my stupid book" and work on my plastic car models. When I was a kid, I used to assemble plastic car models. I even remember working on them during my first year of high school. I brought some of them in for a required speech about hobbies. It wasn't until I was retired that I started again. This time though, there was even greater detail and I painted them correctly. I focused on cars in the late 50's through the 60's. These were my muscle cars growing up. It always brought me a great deal of satisfaction.

As I worked on my plastic car model throughout the day, I kept checking for emails. There were no emails, no phone messages and no wacky people calling me. Things were back to normal for a change. I felt relaxed and my wife wasn't yelling at me which is a side benefit. I guess I'd just play the waiting game. I am getting good at this!

Days went by, there was nothing in the mail, no voice mails and no emails. Thank God the nightmare was over. But little did I know, it was only beginning. My wife headed to northern New Jersey on Sunday night so she could watch my grandson for a few days so the kids could work. She stayed there for three days and I would be home alone. That worked for me, but by the time she got home on Wednesday she was exhausted. I understood, but we are a family and we need to stick together.

On Sunday night, my wife headed north on the Garden State Parkway to Route 287 on her two-hour ride to my son's house. It has become a regular routine. I would settle in and watch the popular football game or a movie. A glass of Chardonnay is all I need to complete the evening.

On this particular Sunday, my cell phone rang. It was my wife and she's in a panic. I can tell.

"Help me," she screams. "There is a tactor trailer about two feet from my bumper and he has been trailing me for ten miles. Every time I switch lanes, he switches lanes and is always on my bumper," she exclaimed.

"Settle down. Here's what I want you to do. I want you to pull over to the shoulder, put it in park and put the flashers on but don't turn the car off. See if the truck pulls in behind you," I instructed her

"Yes, yes, it is slowing down and following me," she said frantically.

"Don't unlock the doors and don't shut off the car. Do you hear me," I commanded.

"Yes, yes, I am so scared" she said.

"Let me know as soon as the truck stops because that's when you're going to take off. Got it? "Got it?"

"Yes, yes" she said nervously.

"Did the truck stop yet?" I asked.

"I'm looking in the mirror and it is very close. His lights are blinding me" she responded hastily.

"Ok on the count of three, I want you to push the gas pedal to the floor and pull out into traffic. Just check your side mirror and watch what's coming in the lane. Ready? One, two three. Hit it," I told her.

"Oh my God it's still sitting back there on the side of the road" she said frantically.

"It will take him some time to run through all of those gears to get back up to speed. In the meantime, keep going fast. I am going to get on the computer and direct you off an exit. He'll never find you," I finished.

Over the next 20 minutes I gave her verbal instructions on where to turn.

"Are you calm now," I asked.

"Yes, yes, I'm better but what was that all about," she said.

"Did you cut the guy off or give him the finger?" I asked.

"No, he just came up on me from nowhere. I was minding my own business in the slow lane and he came up on me. Every time I would change lanes, He would change too. I hate truck drivers. They are maniacs," she said.

I'll stay on the phone with you until you get to Mike's house," I suggested.

"No, that's Ok, I know where I am now and there's no trucks in sight."

"OK, do me a favor and call me as soon as you get there. Don't forget," I requested.

"Ok, I will. Love you" she said

"Love you too," I answered. Another glass of wine was in order.

What the hell is going on? I know my wife isn't the greatest driver in the world and I know that road rage has increased during this Covid thing but this is a little bit too much. It's probably just a coincidence. I was relaxed watching television and I nodded off awoken by my cell phone.

"Hi Hon," I answered.

A man's voice says "We missed her this time but we'll get her the next time,". He said before he hung up on me.

Oh my God it is real. I immediately pressed redial but it's the same old story. It's not in service. Now I'm in a panic. They're after my family. I can't tell my wife or she'll freak out. What about my kids and grandson? That's it. I 'm cancelling the book. This is not worth it. The phone rang again. I look at the number this time and it's my wife.

"Hi" I said.

She said "what's the matter?"

"Nothing, I just fell asleep watching television and waiting for your call," I told her.

"Hittin' the wine again, I think. Anyway, I just wanted to let you know that I made it and everything is fine. Are you sure you're Ok? You're not having another stroke, are you," she asked.

"Very funny, I'm going to bed now, love you," I said.

"Love you too!" she exclaimed

Now I knew I need to protect my family. Tomorrow, I was going to the Sporting Goods store to get some fresh ammo for my pistol. Years ago, I used to go to the firing range with my sons. We had a really good time killing paper zombies. At the same time, it was good to show them how to properly handle firearms. Whether they got them as this point in their lives is up to them.

I bought a 22 pistol in the seventies after a drunk tried to break down the front door in our apartment. I will never forget that night. It was about 10:00 p.m. and I was watching tv. The volume was low because I was always courteous to our downstairs neighbor. I heard a noise by the front door. I looked over the balcony and saw the door handle rattling. I quickly shouted "who's there?" but no response. Now this person knows there is somebody in here but things are escalating. Now he was pounding on the door. I was cursing and told my wife to dial 911. The police arrived in record time and I looked out the window and they had their guns drawn. Next thing I knew is that they had this guy in cuffs down on the ground. I went outside and start cursing at the guy. The cop pulls me aside and said "listen, this guy is ossified. He is so drunk that he thought your apartment was his apartment. We checked it out and he does live in the next building. He hasn't really committed a crime except being drunk in public and we'll handle that. We'll get him outta' here and you will be fine. I'm very sorry but we've never seen this guy before. I strongly suggest that you just let it go. You may find that he will come by someday and offer you an apology. He never did.

What the hell was happening? I was going from writing a stupid book to carrying a gun. This is bizarre! I didn't know what I was going to do at this point. Should I call the cops? Should I tell my wife? Should I pull the book and get sued up the wazoo? I really don't know what to do but I do know that I'm going to buy ammo tomorrow. I'd worry about explaining it to my wife when the credit card bill comes. Timing is good since she's away but no sleep tonight for me!

When I woke up in the morning, I felt good. I would get ready and head off to the Sporting Goods store. I started thinking about prison and whether or not I had the guts to go if I shot and killed someone. Maybe I shouldn't get ammo. No, I am going to get it even if I never use it. It will make me feel better. But how about the discussion with my wife? Do I just lay it out and put everything on the table? I'm afraid. I think I'm afraid of her. I think I'm afraid that she may divorce me. I think too much. I have often thought that my life was planned and I am just going through the motions. If that's the case, then I'm on the chosen path. But what if it's not? That's why I worry. I can't stand it anymore and I just want this whole nightmare to end.

A thought came into my mind. What if I sent out an email to all of the publishers telling them that I was contemplating pulling the book. Even though I have a contract with one publisher, maybe word will get around and this nonsense will stop. It can't hurt. I'm only saying that I'm "thinking" about it. Yeah, that's it! Then let's see what type of messages I get. I wanted the message to be short and succinct so I started typing.

"It is with great remorse, 'no regret', that I am no longer going to publish my book. Thanks to all of you that have helped me through this process." Looks good and fire away. I sat for a few minutes hitting the refresh button but no responses. I'll check later when I get back from the store, I told myself.

I threw on a light jacket and headed to the car. You know what, I should set the house alarm, so I ran back to set it. I got back into the car and I'm on my way. Since I'm paranoid I began looking out my back window to see if anybody is following me. I did spot a black Cadillac which seems to be going in the same direction that I am but this guy was very close. It's about five miles to the Sporting Goods store and this guy was still behind me. It's just a coincidence. I'm in a state of paranoia. As I got closer to the store, this guy is making the same turns that I am and as I arrive, he's right behind me. I quickly pulled into a spot and this guy pulls down to the end of the isle. I wanted to see what he looked like so I sat in the car for a few minutes. He didn't get out and it looks as though he's talking on a cell phone. I couldn't wait any longer, I decided to go into the store.

As I entered the store, I notice that no one looked familiar anymore. Guess it's been a while. I headed straight for the Gun Shop and a gentleman greeted me. "May I help you Sir," he asked helpfully.

"Yes, two boxes of nine-millimeter pistol ammo" I requested.

"Going target shooting," the clerk asked.

"Yes," I responded.

"May I see your firearms ID card and your driver's license please," the clerk asked.

"Sure," I responded. These things were like they are glued in my wallet. I never took them out. I present them and he looked them over.

"Thank you, Sir. Any preference in the type or make of the ammo," he inquired.

"No, just don't want spend a lot because it will be for practice," I informed him.

I understand," he said politely and he retrieved two boxes behind the counter. "Anything else for you today," he finished.

"No, thank you," I said.

"Ok, Sir you can pay for them at the register," he told me.

I kept looking all around to see if I can see this guy in the black Cadillac but there was no one in the store. As I was checking out, I wasn't really paying attention. The cashier could have charged me a $1,000 and I wouldn't have noticed. Instead, I'm thinking of my next move and I got it.

As I walked back across to the parking lot to my car, I saw that he is still in his car talking on the phone. I really couldn't make out any of his features but I knew it was a guy. I hop into the car thinking "watch this". I make a loop around the parking lot. The Caddy pulls out and starts to follow me. Then I make a second loop around and he's still on my tail. I wanted to get a good look at this prick face to face. He was following me just like the truck that had followed my wife.

As I approached the parking lot exit, I stopped. He is right behind me and I can see him clearly in the rear-view mirror. I put the car in reverse and bang into his front end. I throw the car in park and jump out.

"I'm so sorry," I yell. "I had a stroke and I get confused easily" I said.

He rolls down his window and said "No worry, no problem. Go ahead. I won't press charges," he answered.

"No, No, No, I wouldn't hear of it," as I approached his window.

Now I got a clear look at him eye to eye. He's in his 50's with thinning black hair slicked back. He almost looks like a Mafia hit man. Shit, how do I get out of this one? I did take notice that he didn't have a southern drawl!

"Let me call the police," I said.

"No, it's just a fender bender, no need to call the police," he said nervously.

"Can I get your Driver's License Number?" I asked.

"No, no, I'm really in a hurry to get to the hospital to see someone who is dying. I appreciate your concern but it's really not a big deal," he replies.

"OK if you're sure. Let me just get your license plate and I'll be on my way," I said.

He looked a little worried but I scratched the numbers down on my store receipt.

Ok you fuckin' prick, now I got a good look at you and the ball's in my court now. I turned left and he turned right. No more tails today I thought as I drove home rather casually. Now what should I do with this license plate number? He knew I had it so I think I'll just hang onto it for a while.

A few days passed and I didn't mention anything to my wife. I did get a few email messages from publishers expressing regret and saying that it was a good book, but not financially viable. Since a few days had gone buy and there hadn't been any threatening calls, I think we'll call it, game over. But that was all about to change.

The Escalation

My daughter lives on a farm with her husband. They don't have any kids but they do have a St. Charles Spaniel named Milo. He is the most loving dog I ever met and he was always happy to see me.

In the middle of the day, my cell phone rang and it's my son-in-law, Tom. He never called me but this time he was frantic. I could tell it in his voice.

"Bill, I need you to come down to the barn right away," he screamed excitedly.

"Is my daughter, Okay," I asked in a panicked voice.

"Yes, she's fine, but something has happened and I need your help. I haven't told your daughter but can you get here right away? Don't call her just come as fast as you can. Meet me by the barn," he implored.

"Ok, I'm on my way," I responded quickly.

I couldn't help but think that something terrible had happened, but my daughter is Ok. I grabbed my coat and yelled to my wife; "I'll be back in a while." I knew that she would be on the phone to my daughter telling her I was nuts. The 30-minute drive to my son-in-law's house seemed like it took forever. I was frantic but being careful not to speed.

When I got there, I could see my son-in-law pacing back and forth on the side of the barn. The barn was far enough from the house so I wouldn't be seen by my daughter. I pulled onto the grass and jumped out, like a Sheriff making an arrest.

"Tom what's the matter?" He said, "It's the goats, they're dead, somebody killed them," he yelled.

I grabbed him by the shoulders and said "Tom, show me!"

Tom opened the barn door slowly and we walked over to the goat pen. There were the two of them suspended by pitchforks on their necks. These are not baby goats, but 220-pound mature ones.

"Oh, my God, Tom! Oh my God! My daughter will be devastated," I exclaimed.

Tom said quietly, "Bill, you tell her. I just can't. I loved those goats."

"Ok, Tom, let me go down to the house and tell her. I don't know if I want her to see this," I said.

I walked down to the house slowly and could hear Milo barking inside the house. He knew that someone was on the property. I rang the doorbell and my daughter came to the door.

"What are you doing here? Did you see Tom," she asked.

"Can I come in," I asked.

"Sure, I'm sorry," she replied

"Actually, Tom called me and right now he's up by the barn. Something happened to the goats," I told her sadly.

I saw my daughter stare like I never did before. Just a blank frightening stare I never want to see again. "What happened, is Tom OK?"

"Yes, Tom is Ok but I'm afraid that the goats are dead," I said as gingerly as possible.

"What do you mean? I just fed them this morning. I'm going up to see them," she declared.

"No, don't. It looks like they were killed. Not by another animal, but on purpose and I think it has something to do with me."

"What are you talking about? I want to see them," she insisted.

"No, no. Let's get Tom down here and we'll call the police," I suggested.

All of a sudden, my daughter burst into tears and started yelling. "Those are my babies, I need to see them, I Love them."

"I know, I know, but we have to call the police first," I said.

I opened the door and called for Tom. He came walking across the yard slowly like he almost didn't want to come in. When he got to the house, my daughter started yelling at him.

"Why didn't you tell me you bastard! You piece of shit! You had to call my Dad and get him involved? What the fuck is wrong with you," she screamed. The whole time Tom looked down like he was dejected.

Very quietly he said, "I didn't know what else to do."

I walked over and hugged both of them. This is my fault, I never meant to get you involved. They never asked another question and I certainly didn't think they heard what I was saying.

"Ok, let's call the police, we need to do this, I will call them" I said again.

I dialed 911, waited for the dispatcher to answer and gave them the name and address of where the atrocity had taken place. The police said that they should have someone there in a few minutes.

"Let's all go up to the barn and wait for the police. This will be a crime scene so I don't want either of you going back into the barn until the police arrive," I instructed.

My daughter put on her boots, hat, coat and gloves and the whole time Milo was barking as if he knew something was wrong. I asked my daughter, "have you spoken to Mom recently?"

"Yes, just before you got here, she thinks you're nuts" Probably correct on that one, I thought. Within minutes the police arrived, I was very impressed.

The officer pulled in right behind my car. Looked like he was radioing his position and then slowly emerged.

He was tall, about six foot two with brown wavy hair and a muscular build.

"Good afternoon, my name is Officer Fred Daniels and I am the investigating officer. Before I start, I'd like to get your names and addresses please, my son-in-law started followed by my daughter. Then I gave my information and noted that I was the father-in-law who was contacted by my son-in-law.

"Just a minute, let's back up for a second. He points to Tom and said, "Sir, can you tell me what took place here today?"

"Yes Sir, I went to the barn to check on the goats," Tom replied.

"Approximately what time was that sir?" the officer asked.

"About 1:30 Officer," he said.

"Is that something that you do every day," the office inquired.

"Yes Sir," Tom replied.

"Ok, can we go inside and see what happened," the officer requested.

"Yes," Tom said as he unlocked the barn door and put his arm around my daughter. As they walked in, my daughter let out a blood curdling scream. She fell to the floor and started screaming even louder.

"Sir, have you touched or moved anything here," the police officer asked.

"No, I have not. This is exactly how I found them," Tom replied.

My daughter was on the floor screaming like a banshee.

The officer turns to me and asks, "Sir, may I ask why you are here?"

"Yes, my son-in-law called me because he knew how devastating this would be for my daughter," I answered.

"Thank You" "Now I want to ask each of you a question. Do you know why anyone would want to harm these goats," he asked.

Tom started first and said, "I don't know anyone who would want to do harm to these innocent creatures." He then turned to my daughter and she kept saying "No, No, No." And finally, the question I had been dreading

"Do you have any idea what happened here today or the parties responsible," he asked me.

"I firmly said "No."

After making some notes on his pad, the officer said "I need to get some pictures taken and probably call the Fish and

Game Warden as a courtesy. This area will be designated as a crime scene, so I would ask you not to move anything or disturb any potential evidence. I have another officer coming to assist."

The officer went to his trunk and got some yellow tape that said Crime Scene Investigation. He went inside the barn and set up spotlights. The officer told Tom that it was best to get my daughter inside the house and start consoling her. We all went into the house and I knew it was time to call my wife. Tom sat with Christina trying desperately to console her but with little avail.

I went into the living room with my cell phone and dialed my wife. As soon as she picked up, she started saying "What's going on, what happened, is everybody Ok?"

"Yes, everyone is fine but it looks like someone killed the goats and we have the police here now trying to figure it out. I am going to stay with them until we get this settled," I informed her.

As I peered out the window, I saw more headlights arriving.

I went over to my daughter and said "I am very sorry but we will get whoever did this and bring them to justice." It looked like it didn't really matter what I said. "I am going out to talk to the police and see what's going on," as I put on my jacket and proceeded up to the barn.

"Thank you all for coming, we really appreciate it. Is there any news," I asked.

The guys who had the Fish and Game uniform on said "Not yet, it's still very preliminary in the investigation. But I will tell you what. This is one of the most heinous things I have ever seen. Inexcusable to do this to animals. I can't wait to find the son-of-a- bitch who did this!"

"I agree," I said. "Officer, I asked, what should we do next?"

He said "It should be another hour or so and then you can call the Animal Recovery Services. They will come by and take the goats away but don't do anything until I tell you."

"Yes Sir, I understand," I said.

As daylight drifted to darkness, I knew this was going to be a very long night. I called my wife again just to give her an update on the situation.

"Who would do such a thing," she asked.

"I have no idea," but I had a suspicion that it was related to the book.

Hour after hour went by as we sat in the house. My daughter sat on the couch crying, sometimes uncontrollably. I was not a hugging type of person, but I went over to sit by her a few times. Whatever words I offered really didn't matter. Tom did a great job of consoling her.

About 8:00 pm there was a knock at the door and it was the police officer. I couldn't even remember his name but I asked him to come in.

"May I speak to your daughter and son-in-law," he asked politely.

I brought them both into the kitchen. "Believe me folks, I am very sorry for what happened here today. Our investigation will continue however we've done all that we can here at this location. A report has been filed with the Fish and Game Commission and you can contact our office within the next two days to get a copy of our report," one of them said.

"What did you find" Tom asked.

"Not a lot, unfortunately. There was no forced entry and no finger prints anywhere. At this point we don't have a motive but that's where we will continue our investigation. We will be contacting you again often during the next few days as we assign detectives to this case. I would suggest at this point, that you contact Animal Recovery Services to remove the goats from the property. Folks, I am truly very sorry and I hope we can bring a speedy end to this nightmare. Thank you for your cooperation."

We all thanked the officer as he left but now the silence was deafening like a serious church sermon.

"I will call Animal Recovery and schedule the pickup" I said.

My God that sounded so cold. I searched my phone and found a local service. I called them and they said they could do the job at $85.00 per carcass. I didn't have the heart to ask what they would do with them but I agreed. I would even pay for it. They said they could pick up today with an additional $50.00 charge and another $25.00 charge for a call after 6pm. Whatever, I agreed.

I asked Tom to stay in the house with my daughter and I went up to prepare the goats for disposal. Somehow, I wrangled each of them off the pitchforks and laid them on the floor of the barn. Thankfully, within the next half hour the Recovery Services came. Two burly guys came out with ropes, tied them up and dragged them out of the barn. Once out of the barn they secured them to a winch and dragged each of them up into the truck. I gave my credit card, signed the paper and they were off. I walked slowly toward the house and crumpled the receipt into my pocket.

I walked into the kitchen and said "Everything is taken care of." Tom and my daughter were still on the couch. I asked if I could wash my hands. I made one last call to my wife letting her know that I would be on my way home.

As I got into my car, a million things were going through my mind but I couldn't help wondering if this was all caused by me. This was the longest drive I have ever taken. The pictures of the goats kept swirling through my mind. Boy, would I like to catch the bastard that did this. There is too much of a coincidence between what happened today and the other events. Things were beginning to tie together. If someone wants to come after me, no problem, but when they include my family, that's war. I still couldn't discuss of this with my wife. She' think I was nuts and she will probably be right, again.

I don't even remember driving home but somehow, I got there. As soon arrived, my wife was standing by the doorway.

"What the hell happened," she yelled.

"I don't know but the goats are gone and the whole thing is with the police now. I had nothing to do with it other than helping my son-in-law," I told her

I was getting a little fed up with her questioning.

"What the fuck do you want me to do? I did everything I could. Now leave me the fuck alone!" I shouted.

I think she came to her senses and said "I'm sorry, this is very upsetting. Thank you for being there for them."

Well, about time, I thought. I am going to bed and forget about this whole mess. As I was getting ready for bed, I could hear my wife on the cell phone with my daughter. She was trying to be quiet, but I could pick up on every word.

The next day, I woke up and the first thing I started to think of were the events of yesterday. I wanted to call my daughter and saw that my wife was already up. As I walked into the kitchen I asked "Did you speak to Christina today?"

"Yes, I did." Of course, she did! What a crazy question to ask the mom of a daughter.

"How is she," I asked.

"She's distraught, how did you think she would be," she answered.

"You are really a fuckin' piece of work. I can't even ask a simple question and you start getting nasty with me, the innocent one in this whole mess. The one who races down there to help and support them through this ordeal. You are really something," I bellowed.

I went back to the bedroom to get dressed. I didn't know what I was going to say next, but I bet it wouldn't be pleasant. As I walked back into the kitchen to get coffee and I couldn't even look at my wife. I can understand her frustration and anger but I can't understand her verbal attacks. What the hell did I do? I was really getting tired of being treated like a piece of shit. I had no support and no one to confide in. No friends, no relatives, no nothing. I guess I would just suck it up like a dry sponge.

A few days went by and gradually my wife and I would exchange brief sentences. I was quiet most of the time hoping she would realize what a fucking bitch she had been. I wouldn't expect her to acknowledge it but it really wasn't fair. I kept thinking about divorce, but that was really radical. Or maybe not. A chance to start over, a complete change, no more yelling, sex again, happiness, a chance to be me! Ok I took a vow and will honor it until the day I die. At this point, I hope this day was coming soon.

My youngest son, Steven, recently bought a new, all electric, automobile. While I am a muscle car guy, I still didn't understand these electric cars. They have to get the electricity from somewhere and I think that it is fueled by a coal furnace someplace. But I may be wrong. Maybe it all comes from the sun. He was so proud of it that he wanted to take me for a ride. I must admit, I was truly amazed. So quiet, and all digital dash and it tells you where to refuel. Holy shit, this was amazing.

Steven asked if I could come to his house so he could show me the electrical set up his girlfriends' father did to re-charge the car from the garage. Even though I'm still a gas guy, I went to his house to see it. In his garage was the cable and charger hooked to the wall. He asked me to plug it in, which I did and charging was on its way. That was "pretty sweet" as the youngsters say.

On the way home, I started thinking about how things have evolved. I also thought about my kids being the new generation and the fact that they are enamored with electric vehicles. Maybe this is the way to go to save the planet, but I'm not convinced yet.

Once again, a few days had gone by and I got a call from my son's girlfriend Faith. She's a nurse so I know that she's always calm.

"Hi it's Faith, I don't want you to get upset but your son is in the hospital," she said calmly.

"Oh my God, he's had food allergies and asthma his whole life, is this it," I inquired.

"He's Ok, but he suffered a severe electrical shock and burns to his arms. It happened while re-charging his car" she said.

I knew it. I knew that there was something wrong. Was it the wiring? We are going to sue those bastards, I told myself.

Faith continued, "He was in the yard pick up dog poop from a neighbor's dog. Thank God he put on a rubber glove. Then he went to recharge his car and poof, he was electrocuted," she explained.

"Is he OK? Can I see him," I asked.

"Yes, he's fine with the exception of a few burns on his arm. They are going to keep him overnight to make sure he's stable and then he'll be released tomorrow."

"I'm coming now," I said.

"There's nothing you can do. He's in good hands and I'm here to oversee everything," Faith assured me.

"Thank you, Faith, Thank You very much but I am still coming now," I insisted.

"Ok, I'll see you in a while. Come to the house first," she said.

My wife knew something was wrong as she picked up bits and pieces of my conversation. I told her the whole story and she said, "I'm going with you this time. This craziness has to end. There is something going on."

I knew what was going on. It was the book! They were going after my family now and this one was a little too close to home. I wished I could tell her but she'll become irrational and start yelling and screaming.

We didn't say much on the ride to my son's house. My wife kept blaming the electrician for wiring it incorrectly. I didn't react or say anything until finally she blurted out "Aren't you going to say something? My God your son was almost killed and you have nothing to say?"

"We'll look at the facts and see what happened," I said calmly.

"Oh, there he goes Mr. Logical. Need to see all the evidence before you do something," she declared excitedly.

"Ok, he's fine and recovering, that's my main concern. Why can't you just relax," I asked.

"Relax, are you kidding? He could have been killed and you are asking me to relax! You are really something! I feel like I am going to explode" she exclaimed like a loose cannon.

Is this how two human beings speak to each other. No less those who have been married for more than 40 years? I couldn't take much more of this.

As we pulled into my son's driveway, his girlfriend was outside waiting for us. She ran over to our car door, and I lowered the window.

"He's fine," she said. "He's alert and yacking up a storm. I have been in touch with the nurses and doctors and they say there is nothing to worry about," she finished.

"Thank God! Hop in and let's go," I demanded.

She said, "Just let me lock up the house and get a coat Ok?"

"Sure, thank you Faith" I said.

A few minutes later she came out and hopped into the back seat.

"Thanks so much for coming. Steve will be surprised to see you. He didn't want me to call you but it will be such a surprise" she said.

Faith had always been upbeat and that's what we really needed now. Besides it could only break the tension.

The hospital was only 10 minutes away and I knew just where to go. When we got to the hospital, Faith showed me where to park so we wouldn't get charged. We all hopped out of the car and proceeded to follow Faith. Thank God she's a nurse, I thought to myself. Once we got inside, I recalled how much I don't like hospitals. We proceeded to the elevator and went to the third floor. As I walked down the hallway, I glanced in each room wondering what those poor bastards were in there for.

As we approached Steve's room, we heard laughter and I knew it had to be Steve's room. He was entertaining the nurses and right away I knew he was Ok. As soon as we go into the room, Steve said "Hey Mammy and Pappy!" There was a sigh of relief from both of us at that point. He was lying in the hospital bed with all kinds of tubes and his arm bandaged up.

"Steve," I said, "what the hell happened," I asked.

"Well, I was outside walking around the property and I saw dog shit all over. I knew I had to cut the grass, so I put on a rubber glove and started picking up the shit. When I was all done, I thought, let me charge the car. So, I grabbed the charger from the garage, plugged it in the car and zappo! That was the last I remember until the Emergency squad showed up. His girlfriend Faith, added that the short circuit tripped all of the circuit breakers in the house and when she went outside, that's when she found him lying in the driveway.

"Dad, the doctors think I should be grateful for the dog shit and wearing the rubber glove. It could have been much worse," he told me. That rubber glove grounded the kid!

"Did the police come? Is someone investigating," I asked.

"Yeppir, the fire department sent their arson investigation team over. The police are also working with them. We should have a report in a few days," he told me.

"You didn't mess with any wiring or circuits, did you," I asked.

"Nope," I know to stay away from things I don't know anything about," he said.

"Ok, good" I want you to call me as soon as you get the report. I want to see it," I finished.

"OK I'll email it to you," he promised.

"Yes, call me as well," I stated.

"Now, when was your Doctor here last and what did he say," I asked.

"He was here this afternoon and said everything looked good. Basically, I suffered a shock which knocked me out. The burns on my hands and arm will heal nicely and I will see him in his office next week. Relax, I'm fine" Steve said confidently.

"I know because Faith is here. You're in good hands. Can I go out and get you something to eat like a sub sandwich."

"Ummm yes," Steve replied.

"No! Faith said. He must be on a bland diet until he is discharged," she explained.

"OK, for today we'll listen to the nurse lady" I said jokingly.

My wife hugged and kissed Steve but really didn't have much to say. I saw her whispering to Faith but figured it was just chit chat. We stayed for about an hour as the parade of nurses kept coming in to say hello to Faith and Steve. Then I said, "Time to get on the road. I need to get Faith home so she can get changed and be back here to work."

Faith worked in the cardiac unit of the hospital and I always gave her a lot of credit for what she does.

The walk to the parking lot and the ride home was pretty quiet. The only words I had to say were, "Thank God Steve is alright." I figured my wife was quiet and didn't say much because Faith was in the car, but as soon as we dropped her off, my wife started and I felt like it would never stop!

"What the hell is happening to our family?" she asked." First the goats, then this. It's like we've been cursed. Do you not see what's going on," she demanded.

"I don't know what you mean when you say "what's going on?" Things happen. Shit happens. What is your theory then? Did someone put a curse on us that I don't know about? Who should we see about that? I don't understand you! Have you gone completely mad? Am I the only sane one anymore," I asked.

Deep inside I had a feeling what was happening, but I just couldn't bring myself to discuss it. I guess I'm just really afraid to talk to my wife for fear that she'll start calling me names like 'jerk' or 'asshole'. Why am I so afraid of this? What is the worst that could happen? She could divorce me and I would be thrown into a whole new world which might end up in poverty and despair. Or it could release me from these pent-up emotions and allow me to live a new life again. Unfortunately, these are deep psychological issues that I do not understand and I'm afraid I never will. Somewhere along the line we'll probably blame it on my parents.

A few days went by and I got a call from Steve. "Hey, I know you're not gonna like this but the report says that someone messed with the wiring," he told me.

"What? Did they contact the manufacturer?" I asked.

"Yes, and they have never had an incident like this. The manufacturer is coming to my house to inspect the wiring. The police think it's foul play. They want to bring Faith in and anybody I know. They also want to talk to Faith's Dad who did the original wiring. The manufacturer is extremely interested in this case," Steve answered.

"Ok, what happens next," I asked.

"I guess we'll go through the police interviews" Steve said.

"You should get a lawyer. Something doesn't smell right here," I suggested.

"I can't keep paying for something that I didn't do wrong," he explained."

"Ok, I'll pay for it, but you need protection. God forbid you say something wrong. It will become part of the record which can be used against you," I told him.

"No, I don't want you to do that but I can use the help," he said.

"Ok I'll find a lawyer to help us," I said.

"Thanks Dad," Steve said.

After the call, I spoke to my wife and told her the details. Although she was upset, she understood and agreed with my going forward position. Thank God I have some support now.

"We need to know what's going on here," I said.

"I agree" she said, which was very unusual. The only member of our family who hadn't been affected was my son, my daughter-in-law and my grandson. My grandson had been the greatest gift I've ever received and if anyone ever messes with him, they're dead. Seriously.

We made initial contact with a local lawyer but I wasn't really impressed, so we decided to continue looking. Now that the manufacturer is involved, it seemed like they wanted to take over the whole show. They even asked if they could take the car to one of their facilities without replacing it with a loaner or rental. Jesus, we never made any claims against the manufacturer. This was their own doing. I made a few calls to some lawyer friends to see what type of specialist we would need. Most of them said that the reports were classifying the case as a criminal investigation and as such, we will need a criminal investigator. He will need his experts and so on and so forth. As the monkey pissed onto the cash register, he said "This is going to run into money." He was right.

A few weeks went by and all was quiet. I got a call from the publisher saying that the first few copies of my book were getting printed and we could see how the market reacted. I really didn't understand how they determine distribution and got it to the right places. I guess that's why they get paid what they do. I really don't expect much other than the 50 copies for family and friends. I am also preparing for lawsuits, most of which will be frivolous. What I'm most worried about is a lawsuit coming from the Pluriman Insurance Company. They have the deepest pockets. They probably have a copy of the book already.

I'd spoken to my daughter and son-in-law and they seemed to be much better now. Since my son was released from the hospital, things have also settled down. My wife continued to do her weekly baby sitting at my other son's house. Things were starting to get back to normal.

While I was at home, I decided to start researching all of the officers, board members and attorneys connected with the Pluriman Insurance Company. I was surprised that a large number of them resided in my state. I found one of the executive lawyers had an office in relative proximity to where I lived. I thought that I should pay him a visit to see if I could get some information about what was going on.

I no longer counted the days and sometimes I don't even know the date but that's Ok. About mid-morning, while checking my emails I got one that is very strange. It said "Your son's family is in trouble." Shit, what the hell is happening. I immediately called my wife who is at my son's house. "Is everything Ok? Is the baby there," I asked.

"Yes, everything is fine. The baby is down for a nap and Michael is working in his office. Renee is at work and she just texted me. "You know that Renee thinks you're crazy too!" she said. "Why are you calling, what's wrong?"

"I got a strange message saying that the family is in trouble. Has anyone shown up at the door? Are there any strange cars parked outside," I asked.

"No, not at all. Everything is quiet."

"I am coming down there, I am very concerned about this email," I told her. Don't let anyone in and don't go any place," I begged.

"Don't waste your time" she said. "There is nothing wrong. Are you having hallucinations again," she asked.

"No, no, I'm not, but I am still coming. Goodbye," I said.

I grabbed my gun, threw on a coat and proceeded to the car. I put the ammo in the glove box and the gun in the trunk just to make sure I was following all of the transport rules. I got on the New Jersey Parkway and was probably doing 90 mph. I knew it would take about 2 hours to get there. The whole way there I kept thinking about my family and my grandson Luke. He couldn't have two better parents than my son, Michael and daughter-in-law, Renee.

I kept thinking about why somebody would warn me when all of the other messages have been threats. Is there someone looking out for me or is someone inducing me into a trap. In either case, I must protect my family. This is torture, I can't stand it anymore! I just kept driving with the same thoughts swirling in my head.

When I arrived at my son's house, I felt much better. All was good for now. I rang the doorbell and my wife came to the door and opened it.

"Where's the baby," I said.

"Renee took him food shopping," she told me.

"Where?" I shouted.

"At the local Wholesome Foods," she said.

I knew exactly where it was. "I'll be back later," I said hurriedly.

I ran back to the car and sped off like a maniac. I had a feeling that something was very wrong or was it a premonition?

I arrived at the store a few minutes later. I grabbed my pistol and shoved it into my belt and zipped my coat. I went in through the exit and there I came face to face with him. He had my grandchild in his arms. I stood in front of him and said "May I hold the baby? He looks just like my grandson," I told him.

I don't know if he recognized me but he handed the baby to me and started running out the exit. I passed the baby to the checkout cashier and said "Hold this baby until his mother comes for him."

I ran back outside and saw they guy getting into the car. It was one of those black Cadillac's. I raced over and stood in front of the car and pointed my gun right through the windshield. "Turn the car off and open the window," I screamed. He looked nervous as hell but complied. "Put both hands out the window," which he did. I walked around to the driver's side and I said "Move over and give me the keys." He complied again. I pulled out a set of handcuffs, pointed the gun at his head and said "Cuff both hands to the passenger handle. Hurry up!" I knew someone would call the cops and, in the distance, I heard a siren.

"We are going for a little ride" I said. I got out of the car and walked around to the passenger side. "Open the door" I commanded and he did. I unlocked the handcuffs and said, "We are going to my car and if you try and pull a fast one, I will blow your brains out."

As we got to my car, I opened the passenger door and hooked him up to the door handle. I walked back to the driver's side and got in. Then I started the car, pulled out of the parking lot and headed west. Just then I thought, I never put the ammo in the gun and he didn't even pick up on it. Must be an amateur.

As we were driving, I had no idea what I was going to do next. Then, all of a sudden, I got a great idea. I called my son-in-law. "Tom, I need to rent your barn for a few weeks."

"Ok," he said, "how long?"

"At least two weeks, how much," I asked.

"I don't know maybe $200 bucks," Tom replied.

"Ok done, but you can't go in there. I'm going to lock it Ok," I informed him. "I'll be there in a half hour, just make sure it's unlocked."

"Will do," Tom said.

All was quiet in the car and then the guy asks, "can you tell me where we're going?"

I said, "You can tell me who put you up to this otherwise, shut the fuck up!" I exclaimed.

There was silence

And then I started singing; "Old MacDonald had a farm, EI, EI, OH."

It was about a half hour until we got there. Not another word was spoken. I pulled over by the side of the barn, pointed my gun at his head him and said, "you just sit here and keep quiet. "Do you understand?" He nodded his head and I got out and slammed the door.

I went into the barn and found the two pitch forks that were used to kill the goats. Over in the corner was a foot propelled sharpening wheel. This will add some dramatic effect, I thought.

This was great, I planned on tying up that son-of-a-bitch and let him lower himself onto the forks. I retrieved each of the pitchforks and put them by the grinding wheel like a properly executed military plan.

Then I ran out to the car, opened the trunk and got the duct tape. I opened the passenger door and unlocked the handcuffs. He held his hands out and I rolled duct tape around them. "You come with me you son of a bitch" I said.

He was pretty cooperative until we got into the barn.

"Lay down you prick, arms behind your back," I instructed.

I wrapped them with the duct tape and also wrapped his feet together. I found some rope in the barn and started lacing it through his hands and feet. I lowered the hoist which was mounted to the top of the barn.

I started to hoist him up and I said, "you are going to suffer death the same way the goats did. Except this time, it will be more painful and last longer."

He started wriggling around and started to speak.

"Do you have something to tell me, otherwise I am going to tape your mouth shut," I instructed.

There was silence. I think he knew it was over.

I made some adjustments to the winch setting and began to continue hoisting him.

As I hoisted him waist high, I said, "Every time you move, you will lower yourself onto the pitch forks. That's how you will die. Now we have one issue to clear up. And I will only ask one time. Did you kill the goats?"

"No," he said. I noticed that he didn't ask "what goats" so I was pretty confident I had the right guy.

"Ok then, who did it?" I asked.

"I don't know," he responded.

"Wrong answer, thanks for playing. Until I find out, you will suffer the same type of death that the goats did. You see, I am going to hoist you up and every movement you make will ratchet you down. I have sharpened the pitchforks so they will go through your torso. That's how it's gonna work," I said.

"Ok, I did it. It was me," he screamed.

"Wow that didn't take long. One more question. Who instructed you to do this?" I asked again.

"I don't know," he replied.

"Ok up you go," I said.

I put duct tape over his mouth and continued to hoist him up enough so he could see me sharpening the pitchfork blades. I went to the corner of the barn where there was the old-fashioned foot operated grinding wheel. I took one of the pitchforks over and started my foot pumping. "Old MacDonald had a farm EI, EI OH. And on that farm, he had some goats, EI, EI, OH," I sang.

I got the first one sharpened and loosely lashed it to the fence.

"One last chance and game over. Who instructed you to do this," I asked.

He started yelling but the duct tape muddled it. I lowered him down and ripped off the duct tape on his mouth.

"I don't know the exact person but they are connected to Pluriman Insurance," he informed me.

"That's what I wanted to hear. Sorry, there are no pardons or reprieves. I will just duct tape your mouth and up you go. But before I do, let me explain what is going to happen. I will hoist you all the way up and as you move, you will drop closer to the pitchforks. By the time you hit them, they will go through your heart, lungs and intestine. You won't die immediately but it will be excruciating pain. No one will hear you scream because you are all taped up. You will bleed to death. Is there anything else you'd like to tell me before you go," I politely asked.

"Yes, the lawyer was also involved," he said.

"I already knew that but you just confirmed it. I hope they paid you well because you won't be able to spend a dime. Up you go. I want to make sure the forks are in the right position," I explained.

I grabbed the second pitch fork and walked over to the grinding wheel. Old MacDonald had a farm, EI, EI, OH. And on that farm, he had some goats. I walked over to the fenced and lashed the second pitchfork in. "Yeah, that looks good," I decided.

I lashed both of them in as tightly as possible. What he didn't know is that the ratchet would stop before he even hit the pitchforks. But anyway, it would give him time to think. I pulled the rope and hoisted him all the way to the top of the barn. "See you in the next life or maybe not," I said. I could hear him trying to say something but I knew what I had to do next.

The cops were after me and I couldn't go home. I decided to call my wife because it was time to come clean. I really didn't mean for it to end this way but it needed to come to a conclusion. I went back to the car and called my wife.

"Hi, how are you," I asked.

"How am I? Are you a lunatic? You pulled a gun in Wholesome Foods? The Cops have already been here asking about you. They are on their way to our house. What the fuck is going on," she screamed.

"First of all is the baby with you," I inquired.

"Yes, he's here and he's fine," she said.

"I should have told you a while ago but there are people looking to attack our family because of the book," I admitted.

"Are you kidding? This is serious. Stop the book or whatever you need to do to make this go away," she demanded

"I can't at this point but I will make sure nobody in our family is ever threatened again. I can't go home but I will do my best to bring an end to this. I Love You" I said.

Those were the final words to my wife. I am going to end this thing once and for all. It will probably cost me my life one way or another.

I put my own lock on the barn door and called my son-in-law. He answered right away.

"Tom, I just locked the barn. Don't go near it or let my daughter or anyone else near it. I will be back in a few days and I will explain everything to you. Please honor my wishes" I pleaded.

"You know I will," Tom replied.

What a great guy, I thought. A father couldn't ask for anyone better to marry his daughter. I hopped in the car and started the journey to the lawyer's office. There was still plenty of time in the day, so I knew I would catch him there.

I knew the Pluriman lawyer sent me the email warning me about my family being in trouble. Whether he had slipped or wanted to get caught, he sent it from his work email which I tracked back to him.

I was paranoid as I drove. I had my gun in the trunk and the ammo in the glove box. I was not sure if they put out an APB for me but I drove the speed limit and avoided all major highways. Just in case, I wanted to be on the safe side. I don't think anyone had the connection between me and my lawyer except for my wife. God knows what she told the cops but I'm pretty sure she didn't remember his name. About 40 minutes later, I arrived at his office. It was a small standalone building, so I was not concerned about being seen.

The Lawyer Visit

I walked into the lawyer's office and there was no receptionist. I saw him leaning back in his chair facing toward the window. I strolled into his office unnoticed and I pressed the receiver down and said "Call Over".

He swung around with a frightened stare. "What do you want," he asked.

"I want you," as I reached into my belt and retrieved my pistol.

He was frantic and said "I'll do whatever you want, just put that thing away," he said in desperation.

"I said, I will do the talking from here on in, Sir. By the way, do you know anything about pistols?" He replied, "No, No I don't."

"Well, this is a Sig Sauer 9mm automatic pistol and it's empty" I said. A look of relief came over him and I could tell in his facial expression. "This part is called a magazine which holds 14 bullets," I said. As I pulled it out of my jacket pocket. I put the magazine in the bottom of the handle and smacked it with my palm. "Now, my friend, the gun is loaded but there's one more thing I need to do. I pulled back on the loader and said "Now there's one in the chamber" which means all I have to do is pull the trigger and cablooey. Get it," I asked.

"Yes Sir, Please, please don't kill me I'll do anything you say," he said in a panic.

"That's real good. Do you know who I am son?" I asked.

"No, Sir I don't," he replied.

" OK, we're going to do some reading lessons Ok?" I asked.

"Sure" he responded.

"Read what I have written on this piece of paper back to me," I insisted.

"As I sees it, you can pull the book and go back to livin' your life, or you can proceed forward and it may cost you your life. The choice is yours my friend," he recited.

"Does that sound familiar at all," I asked.

"No, no it doesn't," he replied.

"Do you have one cell phone or more than one cell phone? Don't lie to me now, we don't want things to get ugly, do we," I asked.

"Here they are," as he hands over the cell phones.

"Thank you," I said.

I took the phone and started scrolling through the phone numbers called. Nothing looked familiar. Then I did the same thing on the second one and bingo, there was my number.

"May I ask why you have my phone number in your cell phone? Be careful now because you're under oath. Ha-ha" I chuckle.

"I don't know you, and I don't know who you are," he said.

"You're a lawyer for Pluriman Insurance Company. I'm publishing the book about the disability injustices. Remember," I inquired.

"Yes, yes, I do," he admitted.

"You should, because you Sir, you have been wreaking havoc on my family and that's been a step over the line. So now it's time to settle things," I informed him.

"Please, No. It wasn't me. Someone else did it," he begged.

"Might be, but you ordered it and, in my mind, that's just as bad as the person that committed the crime. So today we even the score."

"Please, please don't" he begs.

The phone started ringing. "Should I get that?" he asked.

"Absolutely not, are you kidding me? I am going to have you make a call and I don't want you to vary from the script. Remember, your life depends on it. but first I need to know who your contact is at the Pluriman Insurance Company," I said.

"I can't do that," he said.

"Ok, no problem, bye, bye," I said. I lift the gun and point it at his head.

"Wait, wait. I'll tell you," he shouted.

"You know I am getting tired of fooling around with you. Let me tell you what a 9mm bullet will do to your head at this range. You will feel your head explode. It will go in small and blow your brains out the back of your head. You Ok with that because I sure am," I told him.

"No, No I will cooperate. What do you want me to do?"

"First, I need your contact at Pluriman."

"Ok it's Charles Wilmer from Pluriman Insurance," he said.

Son of a bitch I knew it.

"Here's what I need you to do. You are going to call him from your secure phone. Which one is it," I asked.

"This one," as he points to the second one.

"I am going to attach a device which will record everything that's said, but if there's one slip of the tongue and bye, bye. Got it? Got it," I asked demanding an answer.

"What do I say?" he asked.

"I want you to tell Mr. Wilmer that one of his Board members, Edmund Thomas called you and wants to have a meeting, tomorrow. You don't know what he wants but it sounds important. Ok, make sure you get on his calendar," I said.

"Yes, Sir," he replied.

"Let me attach my little recording device to your phone. Ok it's showtime. One take only, so don't fuck it up," I told him.

I don't really know if I could have shot him or not but the feeling of power was outstanding. He looks at the phone and presses redial. I hear the phone ringing and I am pointing the gun at him like an executioner.

"Mr. Wilmer's office, Margaret speaking may I help you," the person said.

"Hi Margaret, this is Howard Sherman, is Charles in," he inquired.

"Yes, he is, would you like to speak to him," she inquired.

"Yes, only for one minute," he said.

"Sure Howard, just one minute please," she replied.

"Mr. Sherman, I have Charles on, go ahead please," she said.

"Hello Charles, how are you," Mr. Sherman asked.

"Busy as hell what's up," he asked.

"Edmund Thomas called me and wants us to meet with him tomorrow," he informed him.

"What's wrong now? What did I do wrong," he asked.

"I don't know and he wouldn't say. He just said it's urgent and needs to get on your calendar to meet with you tomorrow," he informed him.

"Yes, I have time, but only an hour max" Wilmer said.

"I think he's onto us. I think he knows about what we're doing to the book guy," he answered.

"He can't possibly, but if he gets here and starts asking questions, deny everything. I can't stand that guy he's always up my butt," he declared.

"Thanks Charles, I'll get right back to him so he doesn't bother you" Sherman says.

"Ok, see you tomorrow," he said.

"Here, here command performance. You did a great job. Now I don't have to shoot you, but I will if you provoke me. "Now where is your receptionist," I asked.

"She called in sick today" Sherman said.

"Ok, I want you to call her voice mail and tell her that you will be out for the next 2 days working on a very important court case and will not be reachable. Got it," I asked.

"Yes, Sir," replied Sherman.

"Now we will go for a little ride," I informed him.

"Where are we going," asked Sherman.

"I may look dumb but I'm not stupid. I can't tell you that, but good try. May I have your secret cell phone now? In fact, I'll hold onto both if you don't mind. Get your overcoat. It's a little chilly out," I said.

I used the handcuffs to lash him into the passenger's seat.

"Tonight, we are going to visit Mr. Edmund Thomas," I said.

"He's the Lead Board Member," Sherman replies.

"I know that you idiot," I replied. No funny business. By the way, you don't have a girlfriend or a boyfriend that's expecting you tonight, do you," I asked.

"No, I don't. I live alone" he said.

"Good, that makes things a lot easier. We have a long drive ahead of us so sit back and relax," I said. I loaded directions for Interstate 80 to the home of Mr. Thomas. From my research, I knew he lived alone and that his wife had died years earlier.

After an hour-long drive, we reached his home. It was a huge mansion with very little security. The front iron gates were wide open. We pulled in the circular driveway and I stopped by the front door. I instructed Sherman that we would approach together and he would introduce me as a friend.

We walked up to the front door and rang the doorbell. Mr. Thomas opened the door and said, "Hi Howard, so nice to see you. Who do you have with you," he said.

"Mr. Thomas, this is my friend Mr. Lindstrom who has accompanied me to discuss some important Corporate matters with you"

"Fine, fine, come right in. I must apologize for the condition of my home. I don't receive guests very often; you know since my wife passed away," he informed us.

"I'm sorry, Mr. Thomas," I said.

"Thank you, and what was your name again?" he asked.

"William Lindstrom, Sir."

"Now, now, don't start calling me Sir. Edmund is fine," he said.

What a nice man, how gratuitous. As we entered, I was in awe of the size and decorum.

"You know my wife, God rest her soul, is responsible for most of the decorations. I just live here now" Thomas said sadly.

I kind of felt sorry for him, but I had to bring this whole thing to closure.

"How about we sit in the den for a while and I can make some coffee or tea if you'd like," he suggested.

"Mr. Thomas, I need to be honest with you. I am not a friend of your lawyer. In fact, I am looking to settle a dispute between myself and the Pluriman Insurance Company. I have information that they have threatened my family and injured one of my children. In addition, they have been harassing me because I took Pluriman to Court and I have written a book about the whole experience," I admitted.

"My, my, this is not behavior that is conducive to a company that I represent. I have worked for Pluriman my entire life and have never heard anything as cockeyed as this," he exclaimed.

"Howard, what do you think about your friends claim," he asked.

"I'm afraid that there is truth to it Sir. I should also tell you that I am involved," he said.

"Oh my God, what can possibly be happening," he asked.

"Mr. Lindstrom, I hope you're not going to kill me," asked Edmund.

"No, Edmund. I am not going to kill you. I desperately need your help to prevent someone in my family being killed.

"Ok then, let's see what we can do about this," Edmund replied.

"Howard, how are you involved," Edmund asked.

"Well, Sir, I take my orders directly from Charles Wilmer. He calls me on a secret phone and gives me instructions on the actions that need to take place. I then make the contacts and execute the plan," he said.

"Is that it, Howard," Edmund asked.

"Yes Sir, pretty much," Sherman answered.

Edmund started speaking, "You know I started this company with the intent that we would provide for those that are disabled. Has that changed Howard," he asked.

"Yes Sir, I'm afraid it has," Sherman responded.

"Oh my, I didn't realize this happened, where have I been," he asked.

"Edmund, I have a plan to correct this situation and I need your help," I said emphatically.

"Yes of course, what do we need to do," Thomas inquires.

"I have arranged a meeting with the CEO tomorrow under the guise that you want to speak to him. I would like you to have him confess that the company is unlawfully cancelling disability policies and payments to deserving individuals. I would also like you to remove him as CEO," I said.

As I stood up my sport jacket opened.

"I see that you have a weapon and I must assure you that I am not afraid to die. The best that could happen is that I rejoin my wife in Heaven. Our Lawyer here, may be a different case altogether. I cannot speak for him. You know that this is very disturbing for me. This is not what I intended this company to be. Can we sit and chat a bit about this whole situation," he asked.

"Yes, Sir, I would be happy to" I said.

"Let me get us some coffee, tea or if you wish, some whiskey," he offered.

"I'll have whiskey if I may, Sir, sorry Edmund," I replied.

"Yes, yes of course," Edmund responded.

"Howard says, "I will have whiskey as well."

Once we were all seated with our whiskeys, I proceeded to tell my story of the lawsuit and my trial. I also relayed the testimony of witnesses who worked for the company.

While it was an eye-opening experience, Mr. Thomas turned to Howard and asked "Were you aware of this?"

"Yes Sir, but understand, that my job was to ensure the company did not violate and Federal Laws. I also watched out for the interests of the Board members such as yourself, so they could not be held liable for any mis doings of the corporation."

"Bullshit," Mr. Thomas shouted. "You damn well knew what was going on and you did not bring it to anyone's attention. And now, this is how I have to find out about it? God Damn It. I have heard enough and I'm sure I haven't heard all of the details. You know I inherited this company from my father and his father before him. We focused on ensuring the individuals that were affected negatively by an accident which resulted in disability. We didn't have any damned mission statement or whatever you call that bullshit that the corporation dishes out these days. It makes my stomach turn. Is this what it has come to? The Corporation is making everyone richer and neglecting the needs of the individual. My God what happened? What can I possibly do to fix it," he asked.

I said, "Mr. Thomas, you may not want to hear this, but I think you need to jump back in and take control. It's going to cost a lot of people their jobs, but you really need to clean house. I also want to warn you that this may also affect the bottom line."

"Yes, I figured as much" he said woefully.

"How did you get involved in this mess anyway. You seem like a nice enough man."

"Well sir, I was placed on disability a few years ago when I had a stroke. I did everything your company asked me to do and then one day, they just dropped me like a hot potato. I sued your company in court and won. As a result, I wrote a book, detailing my experiences and advised people how to win their disability claims. Unfortunately, this didn't sit well with the powers to be at your company, so they came after me," I explained.

"What do you mean the came after you," Edmund inquired.

"They threatened me, my wife and all three of my kids. One was hospitalized and my daughter's goats were killed. They tried to run my wife off the road and kidnap my grandchild. And that Sir, is how I got here," I told him.

"My God, Howard, tell me it's not true," he demanded.

"Unfortunately, Sir, I think there is a lot of truth to Mr. Lindstrom's claims," he answered.

"Your child that was hospitalized, is he Ok," Edmund asked.

"Yes, Sir" I replied.

"What can I do for your family?" Edmund asked.

"Nothing, but you can help the hundreds of thousands of people that are on disability by seizing control and correcting all of the ills. Please, Sir," I begged.

"I know what has to be done. If my wife were alive…. Ok what's the plan," he asked.

"I have made an appointment for the three of us to meet with the CEO in his Office tomorrow at 11:00 am. You will need to confront him with these topics and then dismiss him. As the Chairman, you have both the right and authority to do so.

From there, things will be up to you and I will go away, or..."
I said.

"Or what," Edmund asked.

"You may want to turn me into the authorities, I'm sure they are looking for me" I said.

"Don't be silly, I will do no such thing however, our attorney friend here and I will need to have a heart-to-heart conversation," Edmund said.

"I understand Sir" Howard said.

"I think that we should all retire for the evening because we have a big day ahead of us tomorrow. Based on the wishes of my friend with the gun, I would expect that we shall all sleep in the same room so he can keep an eye on us. Correct," Edmund asked.

I approached Mr. Thomas and in a very low voice I said, "Mr. Thomas, it has never been my intention to harm anyone at all; however, I did find this necessary to get results," I explained.

"Yes, I understand about results and I am a keen judge of character. I knew all along you wouldn't harm anyone. You know, it will feel good to get back in the driver's seat again, but that's between you and me," he informed me.

I chuckled and knew Mr. Thomas had the integrity to make things right.

We have one large bedroom upstairs that will accommodate all of us. I think we should all retire for the evening," he said.

The Meeting

When I awoke, I walked toward the window to get a glimpse of my surroundings in the daylight. It was a rainy day and the time had come. I was a little nervous but still not scared. Why? I don't understand. If things went wrong, this could be my last day on earth or worse yet, my last day as a free man. I woke the other two up and said, "Let's get going, our fate awaits us."

Mr. Thomas offered to make coffee. He said "I'm not good at cooking but if you want to make yourself something, there's plenty of food in the refrige."

After we were all dressed, the three of us piled into Edmunds car.

The drive took about an hour, but luckily it was not in rush hour traffic. In the car, I kept wanting to rehearse and I kept asking Edmund if he knew what he was going to say.

"Don't worry about it. I got it covered," he said.

This was making me more nervous, but I still wasn't afraid. As we pulled up to the building, there was a gentleman waiting. "Good Morning Mr. Thomas, how are you doing today," he asked.

"Fine Thank you. We should only be here for about an hour," Edmund said.

"Yes Sir, I'll get it parked and ready for a quick exit."

"Thank you and here's a little something for you," he said.

Edmund reached into his pocket and pulled out some bills folded up. He turned to me and said, "You always take care of the service people. They will treat you royally in return."

My God, this guy had the same values as I did.

Edmund ushered us into the building and straight to the reception desk. Sitting in front was an attractive lady, probably in her late thirties.

"Well, Hello, Mr. Thomas, I am so happy to see you. I have you on the schedule to see Mr. Wilmer. May I ask you to sign in please and your friends as well," she asked.

"Of course," Edmund said.

"Mr. Thomas, you look very dashing today," the receptionist said.

"Thank you my Darling, no doubt something my wife picked out for me. And you my dear, look as beautiful as ever," he flattered her.

Ok, enough is enough, but he sure does know how to schmooze.

"Let me just call upstairs and we will get you up there right away" she replied.

"Thank you. That's why I love coming here," he said blushing.

A few minutes later the receptionist says "Mr. Thomas, Mr. Wilmer is ready to see you now. "Thank you my Darling", Edmund said.

Oh shit, can he say that? As we walk toward the private elevator, I asked Edmund, "How do you get away with that?"

"With what," he responded.

"What you said to the receptionists," I said.

"Didn't you hear me when I said to take care of the service people? I just did," he replied.

Wow, what a guy. As we reached the 19th floor the door opened. Edmund led us straight to Wilmer's office.

"Well, Mr. Thomas, how nice to see you again. Mr. Wilmer is on the phone but he will be with you shortly. Please have a seat," his secretary said.

Now I'm starting to get scared. This whole thing was going to end in a matter of minutes.

"Ok, gentlemen, Mr. Wilmer is ready for you now" said the secretary.

Edmund knew right where he was going like a hound after a rabbit.

"Edmund, Hello, great to see you," Wilmer responded as he greeted us. "I recognize our attorney Howard, but who is the other gentleman," Wilmer asked.

"Let's just say that's he's a good friend of mine and he is imperative to the conversation we are about to have," he said.

"Fine, fine, it's my pleasure Sir. Wilmer replied.

"Charles, please tell me how we make our money," Thomas demands.

Wilmer chuckled. "Of course, this company delivers services to the disabled…."

"No, no, no, stop the corporate bullshit. How do we generate profit," Edmund asked.

"You know" Wilmer replied.

"No, I don't. I want you to tell me," Edmund insisted.

"Edmund, you have been in every meeting that I have been in. This is not a surprise. Maybe it is for you" Wilmer states.

"Let's go back to my original question, how do we make our profits," Edmund stated again. This time even more agitated.

"By getting people off of the disability ranks? In layman's terms please," Edmund states.

"By discontinuing disability benefits for individuals. The whole business model is based on this principle. Listen Edmund, should this guy be here," Wilmer asked.

"Should he be here? Of course, he should be here because he is one of the people you screwed out of his benefits. However, that is only one of the reasons I am here. I am told that you have a secret society of thugs who go out and threaten people and their families. Is this true," Edmund asks angrily.

"Edmund, I have no knowledge of this whatsoever," Wilmer stated emphatically.

"I'm afraid it's true and I've been a part of it," Sherman said.

Both Edmund and I looked dumbfounded as we reeled around to look at the attorney. "You know about this sir and I'm sorry that I had to expose things this way," Howard stated.

Wilmer looked like a deer in the headlights.

"Well, Charles, what have you got to say for yourself," Edmund asked.

"It's entirely untrue, a falsehood and a lie. I have done nothing other than to turn this company into a profitable entity. You and all of your cronies on the Board knew this. Don't play stupid," Wilmer said.

"Did I just hear you call me stupid? Well, my friend, I have a flash for you. In one minute, your employment at this company will be terminated. What you would have received as severance, will be directed to a fund to compensate those who were denied benefits. I will assume your position and you will get the fuck out of my sight. I will call security now and have you escorted from the premises," he said.

"Edmund, please, don't do this. I don't want it to end like this," Wilmer begged.

"You brought this upon yourself. You're lucky I don't call the police and have you arrested. However, if you'd like to push me, go right ahead. I'm ready to play in your league," he told him.

"Edmund, what will you tell the people," Wilmer asked in desperation.

"For a change, I will tell them the truth. I will rip down every mission statement and write my own. We were built on honesty and integrity and I have every intention of getting that back," he said forcefully.

Just then, we heard a knock at the door. It was Corporate Security.

"Please escort Mr. Wilmer outside of the premises and call him a taxi. He is no longer employed by this company," Edmund commanded.

Wilmer walks toward his office door and looked back at Edmund Thomas. Edmund looked down in disgust.

After they left, I said "Edmund, I'm very sorry about all of this. I think I should leave. There is nothing more for me to do here."

"William, let me walk you downstairs, I want to give you a proper sendoff," said Edmund.

I actually came to love this guy! He was everything I always wanted to be.

Edmund points to Howard and says "You stay right where you are. I'll be back in a few minutes."

Howard stands up and looks directly at me and said, "So long, Cowboy!"

On the walk down the long hallway to the elevator, I said to Edmund, "May I ask you a personal question?"

"Of course, you may," Edmund replied.

"Do you really think you can fix things for the disabled," I asked.

"Do I ever," he said as he put his hand on my shoulder.

"What I am about to do is what you wanted all along. I hate to say it but I am ashamed at what this company has become. Now when I wake up every day, I have a renewed sense of purpose. God knows my wife wanted to be this way and somehow, I believe she's behind all of this," he said.

"Thank you, Edmund, I am grateful to have made your acquaintance," I said.

As we walked through the lobby, Edmund winked at the receptionist.

As we walked outside, the Valet greeted us and said, "Mr. Thomas I have your car ready."

"Thank you, but I am lending it to my friend here," he said.

"Edmund, this is more than generous," I said.

"No, it's not. I know where to find you. I will have it picked up in a few days," he said.

"Thank you, thank you" "I said.

"Go and live your life with your family. Time is short, seize every minute. You don't want to end up like me" he told me.

And those were his final words.

I hopped into the driver's seat, pulled out my cellphone and asked Siri for directions home. Getting out of the city was pretty easy and I got right on to Route 78 West. I felt pretty giddy and then all of a sudden, I remembered that son of a bitch hanging in the barn. I worried about the fact that I had not called my wife. Let me take care of that first. I was very reluctant to call her because I knew she would yell at me, but I had to do it.

"Call Mary," I asked Siri on the phone.

After one ring she picked up and started yelling.

"Do you know what you've done? You put all of our lives in jeopardy. The cops have been here and they're posted outside of our house just waiting for you to come home. How could you do this to me? How could you do this to our family. I'm sick of you. I want a divorce" she screamed.

"Are you finished now," I asked. It's all over now and everything I did was to protect our family. You may not understand it, but if you want a divorce, that's Ok with me. I did what I needed to do," I said. And I hung up. Guess I have to go home and face the music.

The Barn Door Closes

As I started driving west on the Interstate, I started thinking about the guy hanging in the barn.

What if he's dead? God, I hoped the guy's not dead or things will take a much different turn for the worse.

I quickly called my son-in-law.

"Tom, I am on my way to the barn. You haven't gone near it have you," I questioned.

"Nope. She's all locked up just like you left it," he said.

"You didn't hear any noises coming from there by any chance, did you," I asked.

"Not a peep," he replied.

"Thanks, Tom, and please don't tell my daughter or my wife that I am coming."

"Not a word," he said.

"Ok, thanks. I didn't forget about the payment either," I said.

"No problem," he said.

The rest of the drive I kept thinking about what I would find in the barn when I got there. What if the winch didn't hold? What if this guy was impaled on the pitchforks? What if he just died of fright? Whatever the case, I wasn't looking forward to it.

As I pulled up to the side of the barn, all was quiet. I got the key, grabbed my flashlight and walked over to the barn. I slowly inserted the key and the lock opened. The door creaked as I opened it but all was silent. I pointed the flashlight above the pitchforks and there he was. Suspended in the air with his head hanging down. Oh shit, this guy is dead.

I walked a little closer and said, "hey" in a somewhat muffled voice. There was no response. I started shaking. What the hell did I do? I grabbed a shovel and poked him. Then all of a sudden, he started squirming. I unlashed the pitchforks, grabbed the winch rope and brought his body down to the hay covered barn floor.

"Hey, you ready to go to jail now," I asked. "The game is over," I continued.

I untied his feet and forced him to get up. I tied him to the barn fence with the duct tape I had left there. I quickly dialed my son-in-law and said "Come out to the barn, I got the guy that killed the goats."

"Be right there, I want to see this bastard," Tom said.

Tom ran across the yard and bolted into the barn.

"Here he is. This is the guy. Call the cops," I instructed.

"My pleasure," Tom said.

Within minutes the police arrived. I had explained that I caught the guy in the barn. He must have been coming back to crime scene to retrieve some evidence. Luckily, the police didn't ask me any more questions.

"We have your information on file, Correct Sir," the Police Officer asked.

I said "Yes, you do Officer."

They placed him in the back seat of the police car and quickly sped away. I had better get home before he started babbling at the station and the cops will be looking to speak with me.

I told Tom that I needed to go home and soon I would explain the whole thing to him and everyone. It was a nightmare but somehow, I made it through. It was probably meant to be.

As I walked back to my car, the rain started to pour down.

This was never about me. But for some reason, which I will never understand, it became part of my life's story. I didn't really need this kind of drama in my life

I was content with the boring retirement, watching television and building my plastic model cars. Someday, hopefully in my sleep, I will have another stroke which will end the whole thing.

For once in my life, I mustered enough courage to do what was right. It was always about them. The ones that would accept what was given to them and then went quietly into the night. I cannot accept that. If there is one thing, I ever do in my life that is worthwhile, this was it. I did it for them and my family will have to decide whether or not it was worth it.

It was!

Made in the USA
Middletown, DE
23 March 2021